NEVER KNEW UNTIL YOU

L.E. Royal

A NineStar Press Publication

Published by NineStar Press
P.O. Box 91792,
Albuquerque, New Mexico, 87199 USA.
www.ninestarpress.com

Never Knew Until You

Copyright © 2019 by L.E. Royal
Cover Art by Natasha Snow Copyright © 2019

This is a work of fiction. Names, characters, places, and incidents are either the product of the author's imagination or are used fictitiously. Any resemblance to actual persons living or dead, business establishments, events, or locales is entirely coincidental.

All rights reserved. No part of this publication may be reproduced in any material form, whether by printing, photocopying, scanning or otherwise without the written permission of the publisher. To request permission and all other inquiries, contact NineStar Press at the physical or web addresses above or at Contact@ninestarpress.com.

Printed in the USA
First Edition
October, 2019

Print ISBN: 978-1-951057-60-2

Also available in eBook, ISBN: 978-1-951057-59-6

Warning: This book contains sexually explicit content, which may only be suitable for mature readers, and references to past domestic abuse.

After the dissolution of her fourteen-year marriage to her cheating ex-wife, forty-year-old college professor Parker Freeman finds herself adrift. Suddenly middle-aged with so much time wasted, she seeks solstice online where she stumbles upon The Pandora Agency—an organization claiming to help individuals find themselves through submission. Encouraged to be a little wild by her best friend, Parker speaks to the agency and sets up a meeting with a female dominant, Miss Diaz.

Greeted at the door of an impressive Miami townhouse by a young woman, Parker questions her decision as she waits for the girl's mother. Stunned by the reveal that twenty-four-year old Kristina is in fact the Miss Diaz she has come to meet, she is dragged head first into a new world.

Despite Kristina's commitment issues and Parker's shattered confidence, the two enter into a tenuous agreement that sparks Parker's rediscovery of herself. Both are surprised by their compatibility until they stumble across the line from arrangement into relationship, and Kristina calls their time together to an end. When an unexpected catastrophe throws them back together, old demons are finally brought into the light, and both women must decide if letting go of the past is worth the future they could have together.

Chapter One

"MISS FREEMAN?"

Parker snapped her head back to her lawyer.

She still had her name, *thank God for that*. Amanda hadn't wanted to go through the trouble of changing her medical license after they married, and transitioning from Professor Freeman to Professor Miller had just seemed like too much work.

"Doctor Miller has proposed that you keep the house in South Beach, and she will keep the condo downtown. Is that agreeable?"

Of course she wanted the condo. *God, this is happening.*

"Fine."

Her reply was terse, and she tried to look anywhere but at Amanda, perfectly put together in her usual designer slacks and jacket. The resident she had been having an affair with for years—early thirties and gorgeous—waited for her in the hall. Parker felt frumpy, plain in comparison in her blue jeans and politely heeled boots, and forty years old.

She cried on the way home, still lost and furious. Deep down she'd known Amanda was having an affair for some time, but their life had been so comfortably routine, and the loss of that comfort scared her, so she'd adhered to the routine blindly.

Monday through Wednesday Amanda was on call and stayed at the hospital—*or so she'd said*—Thursday they went out for dinner, Friday Parker finished late after her office hours, and Saturday morning they had sex before Amanda disappeared to a conference, or a clinic, or some other work-related necessity. She'd resurface for her token appearance Sunday night, before it all began again.

Her mind still grappled with it all. How the hell she'd come to accept this as her life. The cheating, the lying, *the regularly scheduled sex for God's sake*? She'd been so scared to lose the status quo, the only life she'd known for years, she'd just let it happen, and then she'd lost it all anyway. *How is that fair?*

The house was empty, which was nothing new. Amanda's schedule left her alone a lot of the time before, but somehow, Parker noticed it more now.

She kicked off her boots, poured herself a glass of wine, and sat down with her laptop. Miserable, she resigned herself to answering emails.

Somewhere between recommending chapter nine and a review of last month's lectures for the third time, she drifted out onto the internet. It had become a guilty not-quite-pleasure of late. Browsing divorce forums, searching in the sea of dissatisfied women behind keyboards for something, *anything*, to make her feel like any of this was going to be okay.

Part of her liked the bitterness of these women, and part of her was left desolate by it. Her brown eyes tracked line after line, post after post, before a thread caught her eye. *Moving On and Rebuilding?*

She clicked and began to read. Even on these forums among hundreds of others in her situation, she felt alienated, alone. Most of the posters had been scorned by ex-husbands. Very rarely did she find a woman trying to figure things out after the loss of her cheating, lying wife. The responses ranged from funny to sad. She didn't want to go clothes shopping, her wardrobe was...fine, and although slashing Amanda's tires had a certain appeal, she knew she would never go through with it.

Frustrated, left empty again, she was about to click off. A response caught her eye and made her pause.

If you are open minded and serious about rediscovering yourself, I highly recommend the Pandora Agency. Through them I transformed my life and my views on my situation and myself.

The link took her to a website, dark and sophisticated with a definite erotic aura. She almost clicked away, but her eyes caught the first line and then she was reading.

Find yourself through submission. A professional and discreet agency, dedicated to connecting searching souls to their perfect counterpart to facilitate personal growth and groundbreaking life change.

Licking her suddenly dry lips, she carried on reading. The site was certainly convincing, and the testimonials were glowing.

Could I do that? Let someone dominate me?

She blushed at the thought. Of course she'd read the books—*who doesn't like a racy story every now and then*—but that was honestly as much as she knew about...*this.* She was surprised to read testimonials from lawyers, CEOs, teachers, people with professional careers, people who sounded more like her than any of the tire-slashers had.

She told herself the agency probably had a line-up of controlling, chauvinistic men to choose from, though the idea was totally at odds with all the comments from women who felt empowered and in control after using it. She didn't understand it.

Opening a new tab before she could think about it any harder, she did a quick Google search for "the Pandora Agency." She was surprised to find more well written, articulate, and genuine rave reviews.

Am I seriously considering this?

The shrill ringing of her phone sounded. Jumping guiltily, she knocked it off the coffee table while trying to grab it. She scrambled to pick it back up and swiped to accept the call.

"Hello?"

She sounded breathless, flushed, heat on her chest and her cheeks as she snapped her laptop closed.

"SO, WE WERE right then, she wanted the condo?"

Marion squeezed her hand, and Parker nodded, trying not to let her feelings show on her face.

"She wants the condo, the division of funds was better than I was expecting, and as predicted, she brought Emily."

Her best friend hissed.

They were quiet for a moment, both snapping on smiles and waving enthusiastically when Marion's son called to them from the swings.

"I know you're hurting right now, and everything feels upside down, but maybe you dodged a bullet."

Parker laughed, soft and sad. It was the nicest thing Marion could have said. She had pretty much hated Amanda by the time their marriage was over, and who could blame her? All the missed birthdays, broken promises, and the multiple affairs that by the end were so shoddily hidden, half the hospital had known, as well as Parker herself.

"Maybe." *Have I?* "I just...I'm almost forty-one and I haven't been single for fourteen years, and we dated two before that. Starting over just seems..."

Daunting, overwhelming, impossible.

"Sweetie." Marion's dark eyes, sad and kind, found her. "What choice do you have? You've always deserved better, I know you know that on some level. Now's your chance to find it."

Sometimes it was hard not to hate Marion, with her faithful wife, her beautiful son, and great career as a pathologist—her perfect life. They had been college roommates and best friends, almost like sisters, ever since.

"I just..." Parker didn't even know how to finish the sentence. All she had were a million more excuses, complaints.

"You need to get off those sad divorcee forums or whatever, and start working on yourself. Drowning in pity won't do you any good. I love you, but it's been three months."

Three months since she was served divorce papers, out of the blue, in front of a class of two hundred students she was guest lecturing for.

"The forums aren't all that bad. Some of the advice is okay."

Marion eyed her sideways.

"It is! Like today I was reading about one woman who transformed her whole life after her divorce. She found herself and got all her confidence back, and became so empowered and so in charge of her own happiness."

She hadn't meant to talk about it.

"And pray tell, how did she achieve this magical life transformation?"

Parker laughed. It sounded pitchy, nervous, even to her own ears.

"That's where it gets a little crazy. She recommended this agency that has some sort of...domination program... *Find yourself through submission.*" She dropped her voice, low and skeptical. "I mean how does that even work? How do you become empowered by giving up all your power? Sounds insane, right?"

Marion was watching her, her eyes reading between every stumbled line. Parker tried to keep the blush from showing on her face. Why did she feel so caught?

"Yeah, no." She seemed to collect herself. "Sounds nuts, totally nuts."

A soft breath of relief left her.

Roland waved from atop the slide, and on cue they both raised their hands, Parker to wave, Marion to blow him a kiss, until he slid down with a squeal.

"So, when are you going to call them?" Marion asked.

"What?" Parker shrieked. She couldn't help herself.

"Oh come on, Parker. You would never have brought it up if you weren't interested. Honestly, you need to get laid and actually get off for once. How could it hurt?"

She choked on her reply, and Marion bumped her shoulder, taking the sting out of her words.

"Really though, what do you have to lose? You looked into it, right, and it's safe and not a scam or some sort of trap."

God, can I admit this?

"I mean...I did research, but that doesn't mean I'm actually going to..."

"Do they cater to women loving women, as well as men?"

Damn Marion and how well she knows me.

"I'm not sure."

The admission was quiet, and she felt like she had admitted far more with the words. She glanced around, licking her lips, a flush in full bloom across her cheeks. They were discussing this *here*, in the playground at the park.

"I know you," Marion said. "You're going to torture yourself for days and finally, after considering it and overthinking it and making it excruciating not only for yourself, but for me to watch, you're gonna call them anyway."

Am I going to do that?

"In the spirit of starting over, why not skip a step and just call?"

Parker swallowed, shaking her head, a smile tugging at her lips.

"I can't believe you're encouraging me to sign up for freaking...kinky sex therapy."

They laughed.

"Sweetie, I'm encouraging you to go forward, to move, to do anything other than wait and stagnate and let that bitch ruin one more day for you. You wouldn't have brought this up if you didn't want to try it, or at least get more information. For once, Parker, just give yourself permission to be a little wild."

SHE HAD CALLED. Twice. Both times she'd hung up the phone before anyone could answer. Walking back to her car, another heavy stack of papers in her bag, another day of classes done, she had almost convinced herself to put the idea out of her mind.

She could be wild, before 9:00 p.m. and as long as she didn't have to leave her house... *Damn Marion.*

She slung her bookbag and briefcase into the trunk and slid into her car, waving at the anthropology professor across the lot. Her phone rang and she answered quickly, half expecting it to be her lawyer telling her Amanda had changed her mind about settling out of court.

"Hello."

"Hi, this is Melanie from the Pandora Agency returning your call."

Adrenaline exploded in her chest. Panic made her lips numb.

"Ma'am?"

"Yes, sorry, I'm here."

"What can I help you with today? Are you a current client or seeking more information?"

I can be wild.

"I'm not a client. I just..." Her heart raced, thundering, battering her rib cage. *Screw Amanda, screw this.*

"I have a few questions. Mainly, do you cater to women who might want to um, work with another woman?"

"Oh, yes, ma'am. We do have a few female Dominants on staff. Let me check if anyone is available for a new partner right now..."

Parker almost balked because somehow, this was happening, and it was becoming real frighteningly fast.

Melanie came back to her after a moment. "Yes, Miss Diaz looks to have a vacancy. If you do decide you're interested, I would have to confirm."

Miss Diaz. She sounded like a principal. *A hot brunette, maybe a few years older than me, great body, beautiful smile... Would she use a riding crop like the woman in that book?*

"Hello?"

Crap.

"Yes, sorry, we must have a bad connection. Could you tell me more about how this works?"

"Of course. Pandora Agency will match you to a suitable Dominant to achieve your goals. At the time the match is made, you will pay the service fee in full, twelve hundred and twenty-nine dollars, and then an initial meeting will be scheduled with your Domme."

Parker swallowed hard.

"We don't get involved in the individual details made between partners, but more than likely your Domme will have a contract for you to sign in the event that after spending some time together you both decide you're compatible."

"And what if we're not...compatible?"

She wasn't even compatible with her wife after the first two years of marriage. How could a total stranger be any different?

"Then the agency offers two free reassigns, all covered by your initial enrollment, and if after completing the program you decide to return as a customer to be matched through us again, there's a 50 percent discount on the service fee."

That sounded reasonable.

"Okay. I need to um, check my schedule and think on it a little more. Would it be okay if I called you back?"

"Yes, ma'am. You have our office number. Call anytime."

They said goodbye politely and hung up. She stared out of the windscreen, the car thankfully not too hot in the cooler fall weather.

The woman had seemed nice; everything was clear, professional, and nothing like she had expected. Maybe there was something to this? The reviews were so good; she liked the service. It seemed legitimate and discreet, and most importantly as if it could actually work.

Since discovering the website she had dug out and reread a certain novel, trying to imagine herself in any of the scenarios the protagonist found herself in, surprised and embarrassed by how much she enjoyed the thought of being dominated now she was really considering it.

She thought of Amanda, of their scheduled sex and the way it had all become so rote, mechanical, a means to an end. Some of the scenes in the book scared her, yet it was undeniably exciting, erotic. She felt more sexual, sensual, just for having read it, just for considering this, than she had in years.

I can be wild. I can move forward.

On impulse, she unlocked her cell, finger hovering over the Pandora Agency's phone number. Her heart beat hard, a million reasons why she couldn't and shouldn't repeating in her head. The reality was, she could afford it. Her career paid well, and she had been smart with her money over the years, not to mention Amanda was practically paying for it after the settlement. That thought gratified her somehow.

She took a deep breath and tapped the number to call. Melanie answered on the third ring.

"Hi, I just called a moment ago. We talked about a booking with Miss Diaz?"

"Yes, ma'am, how can I help you?"

"I, um…" She took a deep breath. The moment felt heavy, important, but she told herself she was reading too much into things. "I wanted to go ahead and get it set up."

Chapter Two

THE SUN SHONE through the clouds, and Parker's stomach was full of lead as she climbed the steps to the front door. The expensive-looking town house was gorgeous, set right off South Beach, all smooth glass and pale stone.

Everything had happened quickly. After she had signed up with the agency on Wednesday, her meeting had been set for Saturday. She'd hardly slept, hardly eaten, since.

Despite Marion's reassurances that it would be okay, she was horribly nervous. She'd been up with the sun, digging in the deepest recesses of her closet, trying not to notice the empty wall where what little of Amanda's clothes had lived at home were once kept.

The good jeans she had originally planned on wearing, once her *sexy jeans*, were a little too tight now. So she'd settled for the second best that still hugged her legs pleasingly, pairing them with a smooth silk blouse and high boots. With her golden hair blown out and softly curled and a little heavier makeup replacing her usual quick dash, she admittedly felt better about herself than she had in months.

Swallowing hard, she pressed the doorbell, studying the little metal box, waiting for someone to speak over the intercom. *Who is this woman?*

The door swung open. Her breath caught.

"Hi, can I help you?"

The young woman staring at her expectantly couldn't be more than twenty-five years old. Parker's heart plummeted. *Does Miss Diaz live with her daughter?*

Color and heat leaked onto her cheeks, and *oh God, what am I doing?*

"I'm here to see Miss Diaz… Maybe I got the address wrong?"

She gestured over her shoulder, offering what she hoped was a polite smile as she half turned to leave. *I can't do this.*

"You're in the right place. Come in."

It wasn't a request, and the young woman had already stepped back, pulling the door open wider, waiting for her to comply.

Reaching up to tuck a strand of hair behind her ear, Parker thanked her and stepped inside, nervous.

She wasn't sure she could do this, and she certainly wasn't sure she could do it with the woman's daughter in the house. *Will we even do anything today? Is this just some sort of business meeting?* She had no idea what to expect, and that scared her more than anything.

Following her through the house, Parker couldn't help but notice the décor, cool and monochromatic with just a touch of opulence. Miss Diaz must have good taste.

"Please, have a seat. Can I get you a drink?"

The young woman gestured to a dark leather couch. Floor-to-ceiling windows offered a beautiful view out over the ocean. Parker was lost momentarily taking it all in.

"No thank you, I'm fine." She smiled kindly, surprised when the girl took a seat on the sofa opposite her own. *Is she planning on keeping me company until her mom gets here?*

The girl was distracted by her phone, and Parker had time to study her. She was certainly beautiful: large brown eyes and silky mahogany hair hanging past her shoulders, her skin kissed a rich olive tone by the Miami sun.

"Sorry about that."

Dark eyes snapped up to her face, and Parker was staggered by their intensity. The girl studied her, long and hard, shameless.

A black sundress clung tight to her slim figure. Though she was almost a head shorter than Parker, her legs seemed endless, her dress pulled high around her thighs as she sat back and watched Parker watching her.

"I, um..." *God, where is this girl's mother?* "Is Miss Diaz home, or...?"

A smile broke across her beautiful face, something dark and devious inside it.

"She is." She leaned back, licking her lips, slow and deliberate, predatory. "You're looking at her, sweetheart."

Parker's heart stuttered in her chest, and she laughed, high and nervous.

"I'm sorry, you're..."

"Kristina Diaz. Yes, I'm the one the agency sent you to see."

Those eyes were on her again, and Parker burned in their gaze. Disbelief and embarrassment swallowed her. She was mortified. Tears pricked the back of her eyes.

I am absolutely not going to cry.

Kristina was young, too young, and now Parker knew, she was lost at how she had ever missed it. She radiated confidence; she was magnetic. Those dark eyes studied her like they knew all her secrets, and in a way, they did.

"I... I'm sorry." Parker was aware she probably seemed crazy, literally shocked silent. "I guess I expected you to be older."

Kristina nodded, her hands clasped in her lap, legs crossed, still looking totally at ease as she watched Parker.

"I apologize for the surprise then." She didn't sound sorry one bit.

Parker searched for the words, for a way around this, through this, totally caught off guard. Kristina was gorgeous, Parker found her attractive, yet the realization made her feel guilty... *I'm probably twice her age.*

Kristina's eyes glittered with obvious smugness, and Parker was suddenly angry in her embarrassment.

This girl was the embodiment of everything she had lost—youth, confidence, beauty, sensuality—and this all felt like another one of the universe's sick jokes that seemed to be plaguing her of late.

"It was nice to meet you, Kristina. I appreciate your time."

Hands on her knees, she pushed up to her feet. Something flashed across Kristina's face, and then she was on hers too. Instead of stepping back to show her the door, she moved forward. She crossed the room into Parker's space.

Parker wondered for a second if she was going to shake her hand.

"Is there a problem, Parker?"

Kristina wielded her name like a weapon, lips and teeth and tongue caressing it, her body maddeningly, obnoxiously, close in the suddenly hot room.

Parker fumbled for words.

"This isn't going to work for me. I'm sorry..." Her voice was breathy, making what should have been a declaration almost a question.

"And why is that?" Kristina seemed totally undeterred.

"How old are you?"

"Twenty-four."

She shot the number back easily, eyes burning into Parker's, full lips pursed, hands clasped between them.

"I should probably..." *God, what am I doing?*

"What are you insecure about?"

The question shocked and surprised her. She almost laughed, trying to defuse some of the tension in the room, but Kristina's face was impassive, waiting, serious.

"Do you think I have nothing to offer you because I'm younger? Or are you worried what society would think of the age difference?" She paused to lick her lips. "Or is it that you don't want to allow yourself this, you're embarrassed and don't feel worthy?"

She stepped even closer, her voice dropping to something rich, dark, and Parker was caught, confused, ashamed, and embarrassed because something low in her stomach was turning molten at the sound.

"You're a beautiful woman, Parker. From what I saw online you're also successful and seem stable."

She'd researched her? She'd known she was older and still agreed to meet?

"Not everyone is worthy of you, but I'd like a chance to prove to you I am. In a Dom/sub relationship, contrary to popular belief, the submissive has all the power."

Parker's heart was beating fast, hard. Had Kristina stepped even closer? She didn't understand, not any of it. Not why this gorgeous twenty-four-year-old was looking up at her with hungry eyes, not how the person being controlled could have all the power, and it must have showed on her face.

"Can I take this?"

Kristina reached out to finger the strap of her purse with her tan hand, tracing its length, caressing up and over her shoulder as she followed its path. It was an effort not to shudder under the touch.

She warred with herself. She couldn't do this. She felt pale, old, used up next to Kristina in all her youthful beauty, but those dark eyes were on her and she had no clear plan to escape without it becoming extremely awkward.

Parker nodded, shrugging her shoulder and helping the woman strip the purse away. With it deposited on the ground, Kristina was back, closer. The same fingers that had touched her returned to her shoulder. They trailed slow, deliberate, across her collarbone and down between the valley of her breasts.

Parker heard her own breath catch, but there was no blood left to spill onto her cheeks, all of it already collecting lower, deep in her stomach, between her legs.

"You're a powerful and attractive woman." That hand settled on her hip and squeezed softly, holding her in place. Their bodies were inches apart. When Kristina looked up from studying her own hand on her, Parker ached to kiss her. She ached for something, anything to break the tension, the anticipation drowning her.

"I'd like to earn your trust"—Kristina's voice spilled into something darker—"I want you confident, I want you to understand exactly how much power you have, and then I want you submissive for me."

She was looking up at Parker through thick lashes, and Parker felt Kristina's breath against her lips. Her body was alive, screaming, burning, awoken after years of accidental lockdown. She didn't remember the last time her heart had raced like this, the last time a touch, even just soft fingers on her hip, had made her skin burn. She was breathing hard. Kristina was close enough to kiss, and she wished she would just do it.

Her mind still grappled with how this woman could want her, but the charge between them was undeniable, and Kristina's dark eyes studied her like she was something precious.

Kristina wet her lips, and then she was leaning closer. Parker's heart thundered in her ears. She felt light, weightless, and so desperately hot, tight, wanting. Her eyes fell closed right before their lips could touch.

"The safe word is 'red.' Do you understand?"

The barest brush of those full lips as she whispered the words, and Parker swallowed hard.

"Yes."

When she opened her eyes Kristina had pulled back, though she still looked up at her with a dizzying intensity.

"Yes, Mistress."

The correction made Parker's head swim. She wanted to blush, to laugh with nerves, but the girl was completely serious, and waiting.

She dipped her eyes, taking a deep breath, trying to collect herself.

"Yes...Mistress."

Shame burst in her chest, but then Kristina was close to her again, one hand snaking up her body, fingers tangling soft in the hair at the base of her neck.

"Good girl."

God, I like that. Parker's stomach muscles jumped embarrassingly in response. Kristina's eyes fell to them and then rose back to her face, a wicked smile kissing her lips.

"Will you stay for fifteen minutes?"

Parker swallowed hard.

"Yes."

She was surprised when Kristina stepped away. She took Parker's hand and tugged her over to the large window, leaving her standing in front of it looking out. The ocean was choppy, the tide in, bringing it close up the deserted section of what she imagined to be private beach.

Hands settled on her hips, and she felt Kristina at her back.

"Do you find me attractive, Parker?"

Parker looked out over the ocean, fighting between trying to center herself and letting herself go, giving herself over to this and being wild.

"Yes."

She yelped when a slap landed across her left ass cheek. Even through her jeans it smarted slightly.

"You know what I want. I expect you to do it."

Kristina's voice was impossibly close, the heat of her body, the soft tickle of her breath on the side of Parker's neck.

"Yes, Mistress."

"Good girl..." The breathy words made Parker burn. Careful hands slid around her body, trailing higher and higher, and she fought the urge not to let her head fall back as they settled under her breasts and cupped them through her clothes.

"I want to hear you say this..." Kristina squeezed gently, testing the weight of them, and Parker's breath caught audibly, embarrassingly.

"It's okay to enjoy sex."

Weird.

"It's okay..." Fingers moved higher, ghosting over her suddenly hard nipples. "To enjoy sex."

"Good."

Kristina sounded delighted and turned on. It blew Parker's mind that *she* was causing it.

Lips pressed against the spot where her neck met her shoulder, so soft and sweet they almost broke something inside her. A swell of emotion rose in her throat, so thick she could cry, and then the hands at her breast were moving.

"See how your body responds to me?"

Fingers were rolling her nipples, tugging and teasing through the smooth silk and thin lace of her bra, and she definitely did.

"Yes...Mistress."

It was getting easier.

"You deserve this, Parker."

She was pulled, her back flush against Kristina's front, lips against the nape of her neck.

Those fingers kneaded her, touched her, teased her. Her nipples strained, and everything in her lower abdomen clenched tight, aching.

"You deserve to be worshipped." One hand ceased its torture only to trail agonizingly lower, slowly.

"Your body should be cherished."

Kristina palmed her breast hard, her fingers tracing over the waistband of her jeans. Parker's hips bucked expectantly, moving forward to meet them, then back to grind into Kristina's pelvis.

"I want you still."

The voice that had been liquid sex was suddenly smooth, hard, and the effect was instant, embarrassment crashing over her.

"That's right, sweetheart." Those fingers began to move again, and her little slip didn't seem so bad.

The hand slid lower, and her head fell back, resting awkward on the smaller woman's shoulder. She was panting, anticipation crashing over her, the muscles in her thighs squeezed so tight she wasn't sure her legs would hold her up.

"You deserve to be fucked."

The hand cupped her hard through her jeans, and a soft sound of surprise escaped her. It took everything in her not to grind against it.

Kristina hummed her approval. "You deserve to be taken, sweetheart."

Fingers pressed up against Parker, rubbing ever so slightly, and the muscles in her stomach clenched impossibly tighter in response.

"Do you like that?"

Kristina moved faster, increasing the pressure, and Parker answered immediately.

"Yes, Mistress." The words were breathy, drawn out over the sound of her want. She was detaching, falling away from herself, out of her own head, just a spectator in her life as she did this.

"Good girl."

The praise shot another spike of need right down to her core.

"Do you know what you deserve most of all?"

Heat was coiled low in her stomach, her breaths puffing out in time with the rub of those clever fingers over and over the inseam of her jeans.

"No... Mistress, no, Mistress..."

It was almost like a mantra now, and somehow like this, she was picked apart and free. Unashamed by her want, by the fact she was laid open, bare, wound tight, and ready to come undone under Kristina's careful touch.

"Oh, Parker."

The fingers slowed down, still rubbing her hard, but at an easier tempo. She whined as she was dragged just barely back from the edge.

"You deserve to be pleasured, endlessly."

Her brain screamed in response. If that was the case, could Kristina get her off already?

"Do you want to come for me?"

Yes.

"Yes, Mistress."

The fingers covering her moved in a dizzying circle and then resumed their frantic pace, and just like that, she was back, close, ready. Her damp underwear chafed against her flesh, and she wished Kristina would put her hand inside her jeans.

"Manners."

It took Parker's endorphin-riddled brain a second to understand what she wanted.

"Please, Mistress...please...please..."

Fingers closed tight around her nipple, the pressure between her legs increased ever so slightly, and she was right there, panting out soft breathy moans, Kristina holding her up and playing her body like a fiddle.

"Come for me, Parker."

She did. Long and hard, and every time she thought she was done, those fingers pressed against the seam of her jeans, grazed her just right, and she was shuddering, flying, falling again.

Kristina rubbed her until it was almost painful, every last ounce of pleasure tugged from her. When finally, her hands stilled, Parker realized there were tears on her cheeks.

When was the last time I came like that? Have I ever? The girl didn't even take off her clothes...

Kristina stepped back, still holding Parker's hips. Ashamed of the tears on her cheeks, the absolute mess between her legs, Parker swiped her eyes hurriedly.

She didn't want to turn around, her breathing still ragged, body still burning from her. What would she even say after...*that?*

"I enjoyed that, a lot."

Kristina's voice was soft in the quiet of the room. "If you like, I'll show you out now. I know you were unsure before and probably need time to process our discussion."

Parker nodded, running her fingers under her eyes one last time before she turned.

Kristina was watching her, and she was absolutely gorgeous. Her eyes were almost black, a flush across her beautiful face. She was all high cheekbones and plump lips, but the desire in those eyes was somehow all for her. Parker blushed, looking down at the wooden floor under her feet.

"Don't." Kristina stepped forward. "You're beautiful; hold your head up."

God, this girl is intense.

A moment passed between them, and then Parker was disappointed to see Kristina was striding away.

When she returned, she pressed a card into Parker's hands.

"I hope you'll think about our time together today. You can reach me through any of those." She indicated the card. "And let me know what you decide."

Parker nodded her agreement. Suddenly, she didn't want to leave.

"I'd offer you a shower before you go, but I'm only human and I don't trust my self-control if you stay, and you need time to digest."

The words would have been corny, cheesy, coming from anyone else, but from her, with those probing eyes, that desire-rough voice, Parker almost believed them. *This girl really finds me attractive.*

"That's... I'll be fine. Thank you."

She offered Kristina a shy smile, pleased to receive a dazzling one in return.

They walked to the door in silence, and Parker hovered on the stoop. She wanted to say something, anything, but her head was still so tangled with all this, she had no idea where to even start.

"Drive safely."

She nodded. Raised her eyes to meet Kristina's, held them for a second, before, blushing, she turned to leave.

Her legs shook as she slid down into her car, uncomfortable in her ruined underwear and still sensitive. She felt dirty—this was the most casual sexual encounter she'd ever had.

Reaching behind her to put on her seat belt, she noticed Kristina was still watching from the doorway. Their eyes met, and even across the space, she gave Parker a smile that made her burn.

With one last smile and half a wave, Parker fumbled the keys into the ignition and started her car.

At the end of the driveway, she glanced back in the rearview, surprised to find Kristina still there, watching her car, as it turned and left onto the street.

FOR THE FIRST time in what she'd realized was over a year, she'd woken up and gone for a run. Once upon a time she had been an addict. Pounding the pavement as the sun rose had been as vital as her morning cup of coffee, but like so much else, in the monotony of her marriage, her life, that passion had been lost too.

Parker felt sluggish, slow, already struggling and barely a quarter of the way around what had once been her easy route, but she forced herself to go on. She had found something, a little piece of herself in her long-forgotten running shoes, and with every step she took, she saw more clearly just how much she had let slip away.

What wasn't so clear was Kristina. If it hadn't been for the small gray-scale business card lying on her nightstand when she woke up, she might actually have believed she'd dreamed the whole thing.

Marion had called four times, and Parker had ignored every single one because she had absolutely no idea what she was going to say.

Yes, it went great, we hardly talked at all, she got me off without even taking off my clothes—oh, and she's sixteen years younger than me.

Part of her was scandalized by her actions, and part of her was impressed, excited. All of her felt guilty.

She puffed out another exhale, trying to control her breathing, studiously ignoring the stitch that was digging a hole in her side. A woman passed by in the opposite direction, her pace far more punishing and her face far less red than Parker knew her own was by now. *When did I become this?*

Her body had always been slim and toned. Long after Amanda stopped caring to look twice, Parker had maintained it that way for her own benefit. *When did I stop caring about myself?*

She was embarrassed to admit part of her sudden urge to run again was due to Kristina. Maybe once upon a time some of the things the girl...woman...had said might have been true. Parker had never been short on people to dance with, drink with, date in college; she was beautiful and she'd known it. Soft blonde curls and big dark eyes, fair skinned despite the Miami sun. She used to be sensual, sexual, confident, but somewhere along the way, all that had faded, like so much else.

Kristina was the last thing she had expected. The whole situation made Parker uncomfortable. Being called "sweetheart" by a twenty-four-year-old made her uncomfortable, yet when they...were together, she had no idea how else to describe what they had done. She hadn't felt belittled or mocked, just... *Sort of free?*

She'd promised herself last night was it. It would be a one-time thing, a mistake, a story she and Marion would laugh about once in a while. Now, she wasn't so sure.

For the first time in months, *years*, she was out, moving, and although she was confused, she was *something*. For the first time in so long she was living, breathing, conscious in her own life.

I have to stop running.

She dropped back to an unsteady walk and rested her hands on her hips, trying to open up her chest and get more air into her burning lungs.

Her phone buzzed against her hip. She was too breathless to talk, but she knew who it would be.

She was close enough anyway. Talking a left, she forced herself to power walk the block and a half to Marion's house.

LiLing answered the door surprisingly quickly after Parker knocked.

"Lily..." She had barely breathed out the affectionate nickname before LiLing replied.

"Parker! My lovely wife was just on her way out to check on you. Roland and I were going to head to the park."

LiLing offered her a smile, beautiful as ever with her straight dark hair and almond-shaped eyes.

"Guess I saved her a trip."

Parker stepped through the door as LiLing stepped back, and was greeted by an armful of excited six-year-old.

"Auntie Parker!"

She hugged him to her leg, conscious of the fact she was covered in now-dry sweat from her pitiful attempt at a run.

"Hey, buddy! Mama says you're going to the park this morning?"

He prattled to her excitedly. She remembered the day Marion had told her they were going to try for a baby. She remembered holding Marion's hand while she showed her the Chinese donor they had found, in the hopes the baby would look something like both of them and share LiLing's heritage as well as her own. It had worked out perfectly.

"She lives!"

Marion interrupted from the doorway, and Parker offered her an apologetic smile.

"All right, sir, let's get outta here and leave these ladies to their talk."

LiLing ushered Roland out. Parker watched them leave down the walkway, hand in hand, a pang of something snapping in her chest that she tried not to name. Amanda had never wanted kids, but Amanda hadn't even wanted her, *not really.*

"Hey."

Marion's voice was soft from behind her, and there were two mugs in her hands. Parker followed her back through to the living room and plopped gratefully onto the towel that had been set for her on the sofa.

"So... What was she like?"

She laughed as her best friend sat down beside her, eager.

"She was beautiful, and intense, and young..."

Marion's eyes were like lasers, tracking her face, categorizing every reaction.

"Young... Okay, we'll get to that, but tell me first... Did she...*empower* you?"

Parker almost choked on her coffee.

"Oh my God, Mar."

"Let me live vicariously through you... So she did then?"

She was beginning to flush.

"We didn't have sex, but she did um..."

Hiding her head in her hands, she explained the whole encounter in the vaguest way possible.

When she finished, Marion was looking at her reverently.

"Without even touching you?"

"I mean... She was touching me just..."

"Without even taking off your clothes?"

Parker nodded.

"I... The situation was very...charged, and it's been a little bit—"

"Oh my God, Parker, it's been forever. But that is just..." Marion's awe had morphed, and she looked positively gleeful. "So how young is young?"

Parker took a deep breath.

"Young enough that when I got there I was waiting for her to introduce me to her mother and leave so we could have our *meeting*."

Marion winced.

"She's twenty-four."

Something shifted on Marion's face. "How old is Amanda's resident—Emily, is it?"

Parker nodded. "Thirty-one, I believe."

Marion was smiling at her, smug, and she couldn't help but smile along.

"God, stop, Amanda isn't paying Emily for the privilege."

"Are you paying...your..."

"Kristina," Parker supplied. "And no, not directly. I paid the agency who matched us. She does this because she likes it."

Marion sat back, and Parker saw her thinking, turning it all over. Half of her was eager to hear her best friend's conclusions, while the other half almost didn't want to know.

"So you get there, have the realization you're doing this with a twenty-four-year-old, then she gets you off without removing a shred of your clothing and sends you on your way with her card to think about things."

Parker cleared her throat.

"That's the bare bones of it. We did talk a bit while she was..."

"*Empowering you?*"

She shot Marion a glare.

"I may have freaked out a bit at her age and tried to leave. She asked me to stay for fifteen minutes and then... She said all this stuff about how I deserved to be—um..." She was sure her face was beet red.

"Tell me." Marion was sitting forward in her seat, coffee cup clutched in her hands. "Parker, close your eyes and say it fast."

This was something they had started long ago, back in their college days, when they were embarrassed to share something. It had been their ritual ever since.

"It was something like... You deserve to be..." Parker squeezed her eyes shut and spat the words out quickly. "Fucked, taken, worshipped, pleasured endlessly." She took a deep breath. "She said I'm attractive and powerful, and she just..."

Finally able to open her eyes, she looked down at the coffee cup in her hands.

"I know it all sounds like a big joke, but I... It felt real. She told me I was attractive and a little part of me started to believe her. I think it's why I went for a run this morning. I want to get back to that, to feeling...confident and you know? Caring about myself."

When she looked up, Marion was smiling at her.

"It doesn't sound like a joke. It sounds like progress!"

Parker swallowed, uncomfortable.

"When are you seeing her again?"

She shrugged guiltily.

"This woman told you everything you have been needing to hear and somehow made you start to believe it, she has you out running, and she gave you a mind-blowing orgasm without taking off your clothes, but you didn't call her back? What the hell is wrong with you?"

They laughed.

"What's on your mind, P-bear?"

The old nickname surprised her, and the softness in Marion's voice cracked her open.

"I feel guilty. Is it weird that I'm doing this? What if the...domination stuff is bad or awful? I'm almost old enough to be her mother, and what could she even see in me? She's young, beautiful, obviously wealthy..."

"Parker." Marion stopped her, a hand on her knee. "Don't ruin this for yourself before it's begun. Take it for what it is, a way to kick-start some change in your life. Don't get attached; just enjoy it for now."

Parker nodded. *I can try.*

"And as for the age difference, who cares? Who is going to judge you, and since when does it matter anyway? You didn't care that half the freaking city knew Amanda was cheating on you for years."

She shot her best friend a dark look, and Marion held up her hands in apology.

"I'm just trying to say, forget it. Forget what people think, and forget whether her attraction to you makes any sense. It felt real, right, when you were together?"

Parker nodded.

"Just explore it. Just...let yourself have this."

"I know, I know."

Marion pulled her in for a hug, and she felt better than she had in days. With her perfect family, when all Parker had was her broken marriage and a woman almost half her age who apparently wanted to dominate her, Marion was easy to envy. Yet in moments like this, she was even easier to love. She let her chin rest against Marion's shoulder.

"Let myself be wild."

Chapter Three

IT WAS WEDNESDAY before she finally contacted Kristina, a short email asking to meet again and agreeing that she'd like to explore things. They'd set a meeting for Friday night, Kristina offering to pick her up.

It had seemed like a good idea at the time, arranging to meet at the little café a block away from her house where she sometimes came on the weekends to do her grading. Somehow, she wasn't ready to have Kristina at her home.

Now she was waiting, palms clammy and nerves tying her stomach in knots, she really wished she hadn't chosen a place where the staff were so familiar.

Joel, one of the servers, had been trying to talk to her for the better part of fifteen minutes, and she knew she was doing a horrible job of holding up her end of the conversation.

"Ah, Miss Parker!" He smiled at her from behind the bar. "Your ride?"

He gestured out to the street, and her heart flipped. That was Kristina all right.

"Yes, sir. You enjoy the rest of your night, okay?"

He nodded, and she left a ten-dollar bill under her empty mug. She smoothed the strands of loose hair around her face. Though her heart still beat hard, she felt better than last time. Her *new* sexy jeans hugged her hips, and the shirt she had chosen clung in the right places. She felt good.

She knew nothing about cars, but whatever Kristina was driving it was expensive, mirror-black, top down, the chrome lettering on the bumper proclaiming it *Spyder*. Her brother would love it... God, she couldn't think about Ethan right now.

She stepped up to the passenger door, eyes falling on Kristina who was looking down at her cell. Her dark hair hung straight around her shoulder that was left bare by the cutaway shirt she wore. Tight jeans hugged her legs, disappearing below the steering wheel.

"Kristina?"

When Kristina looked up, something flashed in her eyes, though it was gone too quickly for Parker to recognize it.

"Parker." She looked genuinely happy to see her. "Hi, get in..."

She leaned across, popping the door open, and Parker tried not to let her eyes linger on the wonderful view she got directly down the front of her shirt. Was it getting warmer as the sun went down?

"How are you?"

She looked young, her makeup less heavy than it had been last time they met.

"I'm good, glad it's Friday."

Kristina agreed politely.

"I thought we could go back to my place for dinner and go over everything?"

Parker nodded. "Absolutely."

Kristina was biting her lip, watching her, all the intensity that had been there last time still living in her dark eyes.

"Okay."

All the breath squeezed out of Parker's lungs as she leaned across the console, her heart beating painfully in her chest as she wondered if Kristina was going to kiss her.

Kristina reached up past her shoulder, grabbed her seat belt, and then she was moving away, tugging the strap across her body. The back of her hand brushed the side of Parker's breast, and Parker blushed as her breath caught audibly. *How did I forget my seat belt?*

"There..."

Kristina was still close, closer than necessary, and when Parker raised her eyes to meet her dark ones, cheeks burning, Kristina had her bottom lip between her teeth.

"Ready, sweetheart?"

Will I ever stop being utterly disarmed by her?

Parker nodded. The nickname was beginning to rankle less than it had at first.

They pulled away from the curb, and within ten seconds Parker was gripping the edges of her seat tight. Kristina gave meaning to driving it like you stole it, and not for the first time Parker wondered who she was. She was obviously wealthy, sexually experienced, and in an odd situation for a twenty-four-year-old. Parker made a mental note to ask her over dinner, assuming she survived the drive.

Traffic wasn't terrible for a Friday night, and they made good time through the shopping district, the sun dying prettily over the sea, visible down some of the side streets as they passed. Parker let her mind wander. The thrill of anticipation still danced in her chest. She had written down so many questions in her planner this week, yet she knew the minute those eyes were on her, she was going to forget them all. Kristina was quiet, focused on the road. Parker guessed she would have to be, driving like she did.

They skidded to an abrupt stop at a light. Kristina turned to her, a smile on her face. Before either of them could speak, the thud of bass interrupted, growing closer until it was pumping out from the vehicle stopped directly beside them.

Parker turned to see huge tires, looking up and up until she saw a cab, windows down, at least three men in the truck all looking right back at her. The cat-calling started.

"Parker." Kristina had to yell to be heard. "Don't look at them; look at me."

Parker did, cheeks burning. They probably thought she was Kristina's mother.

They idled a few seconds longer, and the attempts to get either of their attention became more insistent, yet with her eyes on Kristina's, Parker noticed them less and less.

"Can I kiss you?" Kristina asked.

She looked at Kristina dumbly for a second, watching something devious play at the corner of her mouth. She was magnetic. Swallowing hard, she nodded.

Kristina reached across the console. Soft fingers skirted the side of her throat, leaving a trail of sparks in their wake. They settled at the back of her neck, guiding her forward, holding her in place, and then Kristina was leaning in, her lips so gloriously close, barely a breath between them. Suddenly brave, Parker closed the gap.

Kristina kissed the same way she had touched her, so sure and so absolutely consuming. Lips pressed long and firm over her own, a tongue brushed them, and then it was in her mouth, teasing, tasting. The kiss felt like it went on forever, and like it ended too soon. Parker was reaching up to twist her fingers in silky dark hair, to pull her impossibly closer, when a car horn honked from behind them.

If Kristina heard it, she didn't care. Teeth nipped soft at Parker's lip, before another light kiss soothed the bite. When she pulled away, Parker was breathless.

Her eyes were black, shining. Parker expected them to flit to the men in the truck, still stationary beside them despite the green light, yet they stayed on her, studying her, watching her, burning her up.

The honking was getting louder, a discordant choir of impatience.

With one last smirk, Kristina turned back to the road, and the car lurched forward.

With heat on her cheeks and that kiss still dying on her lips, Parker looked behind them in the side mirror. The truck was still parked there.

She laughed, joy and freedom and a little bit of disbelief ringing in the sound. *When was the last time I felt so...alive?*

They pulled up to Kristina's house not long after. Once they were inside the three-car garage and the purr of the engine had died, she found herself nervous, scrambling for something to say. Kristina beat her to it.

Somehow she was already up and out, around the car and opening the passenger door for her.

This woman was so hard to read.

"So, tell me about yourself."

Parker thanked her quietly and followed as she was led through a door on the side of the house.

"Well. I'm a Professor at FIU, English Lit."

The house was gorgeous. She had no idea what else to say about herself.

"How about you? This is quite a place for a twenty-four-year-old."

Kristina looked back at her, her eyes promising that she caught the deflection, but thankfully she let it pass.

"I manage an international logistics company, if that's what you want to know."

Parker's brows shot up.

"Wow...that's quite an accomplishment."

They moved down the hallway, passing the door Parker remembered from her last visit. The beautiful living room where Kristina had touched her was inside. She forced herself not to blush.

"Thank you. It's one of my father's companies. Most people stop taking me seriously once they learn that, but I worked hard for it. I've known it would be mine since I was fifteen, and been preparing ever since."

Parker was impressed.

"Is Chinese food okay? I wasn't sure what you liked, so I got a little of everything."

"Sounds great."

Parker offered her a smile. Kristina licked her lips, and suddenly Parker wondered how she was going to make it through a meal with her. She was less nervous than she had been, but the effects of that kiss still lingered.

"Please. Go ahead outside and make yourself at home," Kristina said. "I'll bring everything out."

A sliding glass door was pulled back, and Parker stepped out onto the wraparound balcony. The view of the ocean was breathtaking. Kristina's company must make some serious money.

Parker deposited her purse by one of the chairs at the dining table and stepped up to the railing, the soft ocean breeze rising to meet her.

This was so strange, so unlike her. *I'm out on a Friday night for one.* She rolled her eyes at herself. But she knew almost nothing about Kristina, and here they were preparing to have dinner, and she'd already...been intimate with her. The niggling feeling of being lost, out of control, trickled into her chest. Forcing it away, she tried to go over some of the questions she had planned to ask, about Kristina herself, and about the arrangement.

"You've been taking care of yourself."

A voice interrupted her thoughts, and when she turned, a bag of cartons was laid on the table, wine in an ice bucket and two glasses set beside it. Kristina was eyeing her appreciatively.

Parker laughed, nervous as Kristina approached her.

"Your skin looks beautiful and you look rested."

She had been drinking more water, paying attention to what she ate, sticking to her running schedule, no matter how terrible she felt at the state of her body.

Manicured fingers reached for the railing on either side of her, and she was trapped, Kristina looking up at her through thick dark lashes.

"I'm glad you called me."

Parker swallowed, her body already roaring to life at Kristina's proximity in a way that was as foreign to her as it was embarrassing.

Just when she thought Kristina was going to lean up and kiss her, she seemed to remember herself, stepping back and taking Parker's hand to lead her over to the table.

"Please, help yourself."

Her chair was pulled out for her. *This woman is such an enigma.* She watched Kristina pour them both a glass of wine and pop open the array of cartons.

Suddenly, she wasn't hungry. She gathered herself.

"So how exactly does all this work?"

Kristina paused, a perfect bite-sized parcel of noodles clasped between her chopsticks.

"Dinner?"

Parker raised an eyebrow. She could do this. She had to figure out what she was doing here. It was too easy to spin out of control around Kristina, and she needed to make sense of it all.

"Right."

Kristina set down the utensils politely.

"What exactly do you want to know?"

Parker reached up to run a hand through her hair. Where did she even start?

"I know the website talked about..."

"Domination," Kristina supplied helpfully, amusement dancing in her eyes.

"Yes... What exactly does that entail?"

Kristina was studying her again.

"I was planning to go over everything with you after dinner. I have a list of my kinks, things I enjoy, and I can give you a list of my limits if you'd like. Or we can just agree that our relationship stays within the constraints of what we mutually agree on, and we discuss any additions we'd like to make as they arise."

Somehow this was becoming a business transaction, and Parker was beginning to balk. Kristina must have sensed it too.

"Why did you sign up to find someone through the agency?"

Parker faltered.

"I, um..." She was playing with the stem of her wineglass.

"Lift your head up, Parker. I like to see your beautiful face while you talk."

The command was soft. It made her blush, and somehow made her braver.

"I got a divorce, and I..." Her voice went soft again. "I wanted to do something just for me, to get back to myself."

She raised her eyes. Kristina's were unreadable.

"How long were you married?"

"Fourteen years."

God, I feel like a failure.

"And how long have you been divorced?"

"I got served the papers about four months ago, and we made it official about three weeks back."

Is this the part where Kristina decides I'm too broken, too messy; that she doesn't want me either?

Kristina nodded, but didn't ask any more questions about it.

"What confuses or scares you the most about all this?"

Parker's cheeks were burning. "You. I mean...why you do this, and why you would want to do it with me..."

"I do this because I enjoy it. It's the way I choose to live my life and have personal relationships. As for why I want very much to dominate you, I could say the words, but they wouldn't mean anything to you right now. But over time, I hope to make you understand."

Parker nodded, nervous, tired. *I'm messing all this up too.*

"Are you going to eat?"

The question surprised her. She picked up her fork.

"I'm sorry. I didn't mean to be rude."

"I don't care about the food." Kristina was already closing the cartons, stacking them into a neat pile that she disappeared into the kitchen with. Alone, Parker pressed her fingers into her eyes. She'd ruined this too.

"Parker." Kristina's voice was soft as her gentle fingers pried one of Parker's hands away. "Let me put your mind at rest?"

Kristina took her hand, and she was led back through the house, her heart beating an odd rhythm that made her feel ill. Kristina opened a door down the hall and stepped back to let Parker inside. The sun was setting beautifully over the balcony outside what she assumed to be the master bedroom.

Kristina indicated for her to sit on the bed. When Parker joined her, a sheet of paper was pressed into her hands.

"These are my kinks, some of the things I enjoy and would like to explore with you. Why don't you read them and let me know if you have any questions and we'll talk about anything you'd like to veto."

Parker swallowed hard—all this was giving her whiplash—but she lowered her eyes obediently and scanned the lines.

Spanking—hand, cane, flogger, whip, other object.

The bed dipped behind her, and Kristina's hands settled on her shoulders. She was surprised when they squeezed.

"Just relax and read, sweetheart."

She licked her dry lips and lowered her eyes back to the page.

Orgasm denial, orgasm as reward, orgasm on command.

Kristina kneaded the tense muscles in her shoulders. Parker was surprised to discover she couldn't remember the last time anyone had done that for her.

God, it feels good.

The list went on. Most of the things she was interested in trying, if a little nervous about. Reading was incredibly hard with Kristina's hands on her.

"Being subtly dominated in a public place?"

Firm hands squeezed her biceps, tension draining away under the touch.

"Means me dominating you in a public setting in a way that's not really noticeable to others, but will be very noticeable to you."

She was embarrassed how much the thought turned her on.

"This list isn't as long as I thought it might be..." And it was all really reasonable and not that weird. She'd been expecting much worse.

"It's a starting point." Kristina's fingers rolled over a knot at the base of her neck. "I'd like to get to know you and explore things you're comfortable with, and later we can talk about expanding your comfort zone."

"All of this sounds fine."

Parker closed her eyes, allowing herself to enjoy the treatment her shoulders were getting for a second.

"Just fine?"

Kristina's lips were unexpectedly close to her ear. Parker's body jumped to alert as she laughed, soft and breathy.

"Would you like me to take you home so you can digest all this?"

Kristina's voice was quiet in the still of the bedroom, rich and dark, and it dared her to stay.

"No."

She was proud of herself for the answer.

Kristina trailed down her hands over her shoulders and moved across her chest.

"Would you like to talk more?"

Her body was burning under Kristina's hands, and as much as she knew there were tens, maybe a hundred more questions she had wanted to ask her, a part of her, deep and secret, wanted something else. She wanted to feel like she had that first time by the window again, wanted and worthy.

"I... No."

Kristina smiled against her cheek where she leaned over her shoulder.

"Do you have a recent STI check?"

That was not what she was expecting. She swallowed hard as Kristina pulled away and retrieved another sheet of paper from the nightstand. It was dated yesterday.

"I... No, Kristina." Parker cleared her throat. "I was married for fourteen years."

"But as you said, it ended months ago." She watched it dawn across Kristina's face. "You haven't..."

Parker's cheeks burned and she had to look away.

"And your ex, how often did she fuck you?"

Kristina's voice was rich and all the intensity was back, and it left Parker so horribly off balance.

She scoffed, the sound bitter. Could you even call the mechanical means to an end that had been her life fucking? *It certainly wasn't making love.*

"In the end, not much."

She was too embarrassed to say any more. Kristina's eyes on her felt like a physical touch. *When is she going to realize I'm not desirable? This makes no sense, not for someone as young and successful and gorgeous as her to want this.*

Fingers gripped her chin and lifted her head. Kristina held her gaze.

"Eyes up. Do you masturbate, Parker?"

Her brain short-circuited at the question.

She did...she had. *A while ago, probably? When did I stop?*

"Not recently."

Something snapped across Kristina's face.

"What's the safe word?"

"Red?" Parker hadn't meant for it to be a question, yet Kristina was making all these gargantuan leaps, and she was struggling to keep up, hampered by her own embarrassment, her shame.

"Good girl."

Kristina's slim fingers took the pages from her hands and set them on the nightstand before they reached up to smooth back her hair as Kristina swung one leg over both of Parker's, straddling her.

"I'm going to kiss you now."

She did. If the kiss in the car was amazing, this was absolutely out of this world. Fingers knotted in her hair, pulling her head back, holding her there, unable to escape. Lips moved rough, encouraging, against her own. When she opened her mouth, Kristina's fit against it like that's where it was always meant to be. She kissed her long and slow, then rough and desperate.

The pads of Parker's fingers pressed into the soft flesh of her lower back, holding Kristina against her. She had never experienced chemistry like this. Sure, Kristina knew how to kiss, but she finally knew what they meant by feeling sparks.

"Take this off."

Kristina was breathless as she tugged at the hem of Parker's shirt, and leaning back, she slid her own up over her head.

"But, what about the...test?"

She gestured to Kristina's own clear report on the nightstand.

"Do you have any reason to believe I should be worried about that?"

"No, but..."

"Then it's a chance I'll take, tonight. Take off your shirt."

Parker watched her, all smooth toned muscle and tan skin, and even with the thrill of kissing her still potent in her blood, she wasn't quite brave enough.

She thought about her half-finished running route, her too-tight jeans, and suddenly she was self-conscious.

Kristina was looking down at her, eyes dark, hair mussed.

"You're mine, sweetheart. Regardless of how you feel about yourself, you're beautiful to me and I want to see you."

Somehow that made it easier than soft, fake reassurance might have. Taking a deep breath, Parker pulled the material over her head.

Before she could cross her arms around her middle to hide herself, Kristina was on top of her, pushing her back against the mattress. Her hands were pinned above her head.

"Keep these here, understand?"

"Yes, Mistress."

Chapter Four

THEY PULLED UP to the curb in front her house, and Parker was so loath for their time together to end. Last night had been amazing, Kristina was kind of amazing, and the more time Parker spent with her, the more she let herself relax and enjoy this.

"What's on your mind, sweetheart?"

Kristina's dark eyes were on her across the console. She had a slightly smug smile on her beautiful mouth.

"Looks like you already know."

Parker was able to hold her eyes now. They had found something last night between the sheets, watching the sun rise together over the ocean this morning. *This is going to work for me.*

"I'm glad you enjoyed yourself. I did too."

She nodded, hovering awkwardly, one hand on the door handle, not quite ready to leave the car.

"How did you get into this?"

She hadn't meant to ask right then, but she did want to know.

Kristina gave her an enigmatic smile. She tore her eyes away, licking her lips.

"After I went through the agency and completed a program with another Domme, I realized this was who I wanted to be."

"Wait..." *Kristina used to be someone's sub?*

"Call me, sweetheart. We still have to sign the papers. Nothing serious—just NDAs for us both, and you should plan a visit to the clinic."

Parker recognized the deflection but let it pass.

"Okay."

This was it, time for her to go. *Should I lean over and kiss her? Would Kristina want that?*

Kristina was laughing.

"What?" Parker couldn't help but laugh with her.

"Do you want something, Parker?"

God, that voice. She had come to know it last night, intimately, rich and dark and full of a million promises. The effect it had on her body, still sore from the previous night, was embarrassing.

"I'd like to kiss you goodbye."

Her eyes found the floorboard, the request quiet. Kristina tipped her chin with her fingers until she was holding Parker's gaze.

"Then ask me."

She swallowed, part of her aware they were parked right in front of her house in the middle of the street, yet whatever magic Kristina had still sucked her in, swallowed her.

"May I kiss you goodbye, Mistress?"

A smile broke on Kristina's face.

"You may."

She sat still in her seat, her dark eyes daring Parker. Biting her lip, fighting a smile, Parker leaned over the console slowly, watching Kristina's eyes until her own fell closed.

Even with a quarter of an inch between them, Kristina didn't move. She was really going to make Parker kiss her. Closing the gap, Parker pressed her lips over

Kristina's soft ones, sucking lightly on her bottom one, tasting it with her tongue, pleased when they parted for her.

Kristina was quiet against her, soft and responsive, and it was so easy to lose herself in kissing her, tracing the curve of her jaw, feeling the fine hair at the base of her neck.

Their tongues moved together, and Parker wished desperately for the console to melt so she could be pressed against her, on top of her, inside of her. A dog barked and she came back to herself. With one last quick kiss, she pulled away, a blush growing on her cheeks.

She was pleased to see Kristina was just as breathless as she felt.

"Like that?"

I did. She could maybe see now why Kristina liked being on top so much.

"Yes, Mistress."

She was rewarded for using the title with another beautiful smile.

"Off you go, Professor. If you stay any longer I'm going to end up shirking all my responsibilities and taking you home to have my wicked way with you, again."

Something in her stomach clenched at the thought. Forcing herself to get a hold of herself, Parker swung open the door and clambered up and out of the car.

"You're working today?"

Kristina nodded, something dark still in her eyes.

"Come here."

Parker rolled her eyes playfully, but dutifully dropped her purse on the curb and moved to the driver side of the car.

"All the way."

Kristina beckoned her to lean down with a crook of her index fingers.

"Next time you roll your eyes at me, I'm going to spank you. Do you understand?"

Parker's heart raced. She couldn't find the gumption to look contrite when she was actually excited at the prospect.

"No, sweetheart, it won't be for your pleasure. Not until you've repented for your sins anyway."

Kristina caught the collar of her shirt and pulled her back in for a rough kiss. By the time she was released, Parker was gripping the shiny door of the car for support, embarrassingly hot, a mess between her legs, again.

"I enjoyed last night, a lot, and this morning." Kristina offered the words with a salacious smile. "Call me, okay?"

Parker promised she would, reluctantly stepping away and picking up her purse. She watched as the car pulled away from the curb with a roar, until it had disappeared out of sight.

Wow.

She was still floating on cloud nine while she dug through her purse for her cell, and hit Marion's speed dial.

"You're alive!"

She took a deep breath. She felt light. She felt young and free, and happy in a way she hadn't been in so long.

"I'm alive, and the reviews were true, all of them. It's amazing, and she's sort of amazing."

"Oh my God, you did it! I'm old and married. Give me details!"

Marion was half shrieking, and Parker heard LiLing laughing in the background. Parker started up the path, still digging in her purse for her keys while she held the phone against her ear with her shoulder.

"Well, she took me to bed, tied me to the headboard, and gave me the best orgasm of my life, and then gave me about four more that were just as good. We drank champagne at midnight and watched the sun rise in the morning. That was between rounds two and three... I just..."

She was smiling. She dumped her keys in the bowl on the side table.

"It was good, M. So good."

Marion was squealing. All the giddy joy Parker had shared with her best friend a second before turned to ice in her stomach.

A loud thud sounded upstairs.

"M... Marion..." She hissed down the phone, frozen behind the front door. "There's someone in the house. I just got home..."

A high, long note sounded above her, almost like singing.

"...rker, just leave... Call the cops."

"I'm going up... It sounds like... People talking, I don't know."

She was already padding up the stairs, heels kicked off in the hall. She heard Marion down the line telling LiLing to go. The thought that LiLing would be here soon offered some comfort. *What the hell is going on?*

As she stepped into the upstairs hall, her heart was in her throat, fear prickling across her forearms, leaving goose bumps in its wake.

Marion was yelling her name down the phone, over and over, but it stayed held loose in her fist at her side.

A long moan sounded and she felt sick.

The door to her bedroom was ajar, and she pushed it open. The ice in her veins shattered.

"What *the fuck* are you doing?"

The words were vicious, snarled, feral, and anger exploded in her chest. Was the universe seriously not done with her? Hadn't it taunted her enough?

"Shit, Parker..."

Amanda shoved Emily off her, Emily scrabbling to cover herself with *Parker's* comforter, which only infuriated her more.

"What the fuck are you doing here?" She roared the words, angry to the point of tears, because of course, of course things couldn't be good and easy and mending. Amanda had to fuck it all up, again.

"You need to calm down." Amanda was on her feet, that stupid, reasonable doctor mask on her face, hands out as if to soothe her.

Fuck her.

"Calm down? Calm fucking down? You're in *my* house, in *my* bed, fucking the woman you broke up our marriage for, and you're asking *me* to calm down?"

Amanda ran her hands through her hair, her eyes wide like Parker was the crazy one in all this.

"Jesus... Parker, you were supposed to be at the coffee shop this morning doing your grading for the weekend, as usual."

She isn't even sorry, only sorry she's been caught.

"My schedule changed." She grit out the words.

Behind Amanda, Emily was tugging on her clothes in a hurry.

"Look, I just came to get the last of my stuff."

Is she for fucking real?

"Oh, this stuff?"

Parker stormed down the hall, not waiting for either of them to follow. She threw open the window in the spare bedroom where she had shoved what little remained of Amanda's things.

She tore open a box and it felt good. She smashed three vinyl albums over her knee, and it felt better.

"Here's your motherfucking stuff, Amanda!"

God, I needed this.

Broken vinyl littered the yard below like paper. More followed.

A hand grabbed her arm. Amanda was dressed now, and Parker had never seen her like this. Perhaps before she really hadn't felt anything for her at all, because now, her blue eyes burned, and Parker wondered if she was going to hit her. Part of her wanted her to.

"Take your hands off her. The cops are already on their way, Amanda."

LiLing was standing in the doorway, breathless, Emily held back behind her arm.

Parker shrugged the hand off her bicep, hard.

"That's right, *Amanda*, take your hands off me, and go back to your perfect little life with your perfect little *slut*." She spat the words before lifting the entire box of records and chucking it out of the window.

"You crazy bitch!" Amanda was wringing her hands, running her fingers through her hair. LiLing was talking quietly into her cell, and Parker just couldn't stop. She lost herself in the routine: lift, turn, toss it out of the window.

When the last box hit the yard below with a satisfying smash, she turned back to the room, her voice raw.

"There's your fucking stuff. Now get the *fuck* out of my house."

IN HINDSIGHT, SHE could have handled things better.

She was sitting on Marion's sofa, still wearing the same shirt Kristina had peeled off her last night. That felt so long ago now. *What was I doing?*

Her phone buzzed beside her.

"Want me to check it?"

She nodded, grateful for Marion, for LiLing who she could hear in the kitchen entertaining Roland while they once again dealt with the fallout from her shitty life.

"Okay, it's a reply from the lawyer..." Marion was silent as she read, and Parker just let her head fall into her hands.

"When you settled, the house and all property in it became yours... So she can't go after you for the vinyl and her other shit. Legal speak, legal speak... In the event that you wish to press charges for trespassing, it would be an airtight case given there's already a police report detailing her presence on the property. It would also not be hard to prove breaking and entering... Parker?"

Marion was waiting for a response, but Parker couldn't even bring herself to lift her head. *What the hell was I doing?* She wasn't the person who just flipped out and started tossing things out of the window.

Then again, she never thought she'd be the person to come home from being casually dominated by a woman almost half her age to find her wife—*ex-wife*—having sex with the woman she'd left her for, in the bed that was once theirs.

"Parker... It's fine. She was just blowing hot air. No one is getting sued unless you decide to go after her."

The couch dipped beside her, and a hand settled on her knee.

"Are you going to go after her? God knows she deserves it."

She let the heels of her hands dig into her eyes, scrubbing hard, searching for clarity that never came.

"I don't know... I just..."

She knew the tears were audible in her voice. Marion's tone was soft as she spoke to her.

"Sweetie... Come on. You were doing so well."

Was I?

"What am I doing, Marion? All this...just... It isn't like me. I don't even know who *me* is anymore."

Her best friend's eyes searched her face as she finally lifted her head. Parker wondered what she saw there.

"It's going to take time. You know that, right?"

She nodded pitifully.

"You were so happy on the phone. Do you want to talk about that some more?"

She shook her head. She couldn't think about Kristina, not after all this. Everything was spinning out of control, and she realized she had been stupid to ever think it could be so simple.

"Do you want to talk more about the bitch?"

"She was my wife for fourteen years, M."

She didn't even know why she was defending her now. Marion was totally right. Amanda was a bitch. Maybe it had just become habit after dealing with her bad behavior for so long.

She could physically feel the effort it took for Marion to bite her lip. A beat passed and she wanted to apologize, but somehow she couldn't find her voice.

"Do you want me to come back to the house with you and help sterilize your bed, or we could burn it? Lily's really gotten into pyrotechnics since we built the fire pit."

She squeezed out a smile. Marion was trying so hard, and she didn't deserve any of it. Parker just wanted things to be better; she wanted to be put together, and less messy, less broken. Next to Marion she was always flawed, always the best friend who got the raw deal while the other got her happily ever after.

"I don't want to interrupt your weekend with your family."

She swallowed the lump in her throat. Marion scoffed, turning to call out of the room.

"Lily, honey, can you and Roland get your shoes on? We're going to Parker's."

When Marion turned back to her, fierce love burned in her eyes, and as lost and drifting as Parker felt, somehow it still reached her.

"Parker, you *are* our family. Now get your shoes on too."

Chapter Five

IT WAS A pretty day for a party, though everyone wore sweaters. Marion's backyard looked like a daycare center, at least twenty children under the age of seven taking up the space. Roland was thrilled. Shy as he could be, today, he didn't seem to mind being the center of attention.

Parker watched her best friend from her spot by the stereo system. Even picking up spilled cups and walking kids one after the next to the bathroom, she looked happy. Life had been good to Marion, and she was glad.

The playlist finished, and she quickly switched to the next, thankful to have something to do. Up on the deck, around the fence, a few of the parents who had stayed lingered. When she was surrounded by families, happy, successful, enjoying the celebratory mood, it was hard not to feel obviously, painfully, alone.

Fucking Amanda.

She hadn't pressed charges for her trespassing in the end. Why prolong the back and forth? She knew the woman, and she just didn't want to deal with the backlash. Better to let it die and hope this time, it really would.

She still couldn't sleep in her bed, and the one in the guest room gave her a crick in her back. She stretched painfully, bitter.

A little girl tripped a few feet away. Parker was halfway up and to her feet, but the girl's mom was faster. Something inside her tugged at the sight of them.

She'd always thought she'd have kids, barely realizing it was too late until it was. She'd thought she'd been the bigger person, noble somehow, when Amanda had told her she didn't want them and she had chosen to stand by her marriage anyway. Now she just felt like even more of a failure. She'd given up so much for someone who, in the end, had given her up anyway.

"How's DJ duty treating you, Auntie Parker?"

Marion plopped down beside her and tossed her a bottle of water before she cracked open one of her own.

"Good, no major issues so far."

She heard the strain in her own voice and tried to shake it off.

"Did you call her? Text her? Anything?"

She shook her head. Kristina was another enigma, another decision she was suddenly wary to make. *Look at her history.*

"Wanna talk about it?"

Parker had no idea what she would say.

"You should be out there having fun; it's your son's birthday. Go hug your wife and wipe up some more spills. I can hold things down over here."

She offered Marion what she hoped was a reassuring smile.

"Parker, you're miserable. I'm also tired and I tagged Lily onto bathroom duty so..."

Parker picked at the grass around her feet.

"You were so happy, and you were suddenly making progress. I hate to see you stop."

"I'm still running, every morning except Thursdays."

She heard her best friend take a breath.

"But you're miserable again. For a minute there you had your sparkle back. I love you and I want that for you."

Children shrieked. She was such a lousy best friend. Marion was always stuck dealing with her tattered life when she should just be enjoying her great one. She had never felt like more of a burden than she did lately.

"What made you change your mind about Kristina?"

Parker swallowed.

"I don't know. It was good, but it's also limited. It's just sex. What if I want to date or talk, or build something more than a physical relationship? Which long-term, I know I do."

The next song louder than the others had been, she lowered the volume slightly.

"I just don't know, M. I have this horrible track record for making these poor decisions, and I don't trust my judgment right now. I mean kinky sex therapy with a twenty-four-year-old is hardly the standard protocol..."

"Parker..." Marion was laughing, disbelief in the sound. "Since when do you care about standard protocol? And all these bad decisions you're talking about, the majority of them were Amanda's."

Even though it was almost true, Parker knew the fatal decision had been her own. She'd chosen to stay, to ignore it, to bury her head in the sand until the hourglass was empty.

"Didn't you enjoy talking to Kristina?"

She had. Kristina was surprisingly mature for her age, and for what little conversation they'd had, Parker liked her fire and her outlook on life. Besides not being able to commit and call her, she had thought about her on and off, *way too much*, all week.

Despite the morning-after fiasco with Amanda, the night was still one of the best in her recent history. She wanted to know more about Kristina, she definitely wanted to explore the physical side of things with her more too, yet somehow, she couldn't bring herself to make another decision. She felt frozen.

"Parker?"

She realized she hadn't answered.

"What, no, yeah. I did, I really did." She rubbed her hands up and down her jeans. "I just...don't know. There's no perfect answer."

Marion nodded. Together they watched Roland running with a group of kids, his curly brown hair bouncing around his little head.

"If you don't want to continue things with her, it's your call. But you have to trust yourself either way, sweetie. Don't let all the bad choices Amanda made take away from your confidence in your own ability to make good ones."

Is that what I'm doing?

"Also, you're not going to find someone perfect right off the bat. If you meet someone who makes you feel good, and treats you well, and makes you want to try, maybe that can be enough for right now. Make sure you're not using this idea of perfection to sabotage yourself, because we both know it doesn't exist."

It was good advice, but she was still lost and unable to shake the feeling. Maybe she just needed a good night's sleep. *Maybe I just need to talk to Kristina.*

"I think it's time to do the cake, and then we can start to wrap things up in the next half hour, thank God."

Parker couldn't help but laugh. Marion patted her leg.

"You'll figure it out, P-bear. Just give yourself time and trust your intuition. It's been good all these years about everything except that woman."

With a final squeeze of Parker's knee, Marion was up. She snagged her wife and dragged her with her toward the kitchen, no doubt to retrieve Roland's special monkey-themed birthday cake.

Parker watched her go, and found herself wondering what Kristina would think of all this.

HER STUDY CLASS was filing out, and Parker flopped behind her desk, glad to see Friday. She couldn't help but think back to two Fridays ago—*has it been so long?*—when she was finishing this same class, and rushing to leave campus to get home and get ready to meet Kristina.

Marion had been right. Somewhere between the surprise from Amanda and her shock at her own behavior, her own sense of slipping control, she had let herself fall back down her well. She still ran, yet somehow, she didn't feel the change in her body. Her route got easier, she didn't spend most of the day hobbling around sore now, but she still didn't feel strong, healthy, *better,* like she knew she should.

Her presentation from the last hour was still on her laptop screen. Clicking away, she opened up a Google search, knowing already what she would type.

Kristina Diaz looked the same in the search bar as it had the tens of other times she had reached this point in the last week. Why did she feel weird about looking her up? Kristina had obviously researched her. Parker had googled herself and been horrified that the first result was her staff page at MIU. *I have to get that picture updated.*

She hit Enter.

She was surprised when a few thumbnails, all showing the Kristina she knew, popped up across the top of the page. The first website belonged to some business magazine. She clicked it and scanned the lines—Kristina Diaz, CEO and managing partner of Logistica Logistics.

The article ended with an image of Kristina in a very snappy business suit, and an older man beside her. She was beautiful with her hair pulled back, makeup just a tad darker than Parker would consider polite for business. Even in the clearly candid shot, she oozed the same sensuality Parker had come to know.

She clicked away and went to the images page, *because screw it*. Kristina was actually sort of famous, at least in the business world. It was clear from some of the taglines attached to the pictures there were very mixed views about her. While some sang her praises for her forward-thinking approach to business and transparency, others claimed she was a spoiled little girl gifted the global organization by her father and would no doubt crash and burn.

Parker indulged herself, scrolling shamelessly through the pictures until the results became less and less accurate.

Her thing with Kristina had seemed like the start of something good, and even though she'd not been able to bring herself to contact her, she hadn't stopped thinking about her. Her cheeks pinked as she remembered how many times she'd touched herself while thinking about that night. She'd masturbated more in the last two weeks than she'd wager she had in the previous ten years. *God, I was an idiot for running.*

Kristina had awoken something inside her, and she knew with dazzling clarity that she didn't want to go back to sleep.

Clicking away, she pulled up her email program. She already knew Kristina's email address by heart, a side effect of the number of times she'd dug the card out of her purse to call, or just to remind herself it was real.

Taking a deep breath, she typed.

> *Dear Kristina,*
>
> *I apologize for the long delay in response. Some things came up which I had to take care of and threw me for a bit of a loop. Hope you can forgive me.*
>
> *I very much enjoyed our time together a few weekends back. Hoping we can meet again soon and finalize details to continue.*
>
> *Hope all is well with you and your company,*
>
> *Parker*

She reread the message, three times. It sounded stiffer than she had meant it to, formal. Running a nail across her lip, she thought for a second and then added a final line.

> *P.S. I understand my long absence was probably unexpected. I'm happy to repent for my sins as needed.*

She smashed the Send button before she could change her mind, completely terrified and absolutely elated with herself.

"MA'AM, DO YOU need help?" The assistant called out to her again.

"I'm fine, thank you."

She lay there, looking up at the plain white ceiling in the store. *Definitely too firm.*

With an effort, she pushed herself up, took three steps to the left, and flopped down onto the next mattress. If she was going to spend an obnoxious amount of money on a new bed, she was going to try them all out first and make sure it was right.

She was hoping Kristina would have called by now. She'd gone home from campus giddy last night, excited again, finally sure in her decision to continue things with her.

All day today she'd thought about calling, going as far as saving Kristina's number in her cell. Yet every time she almost pressed to dial, she stopped herself. She needed to play it cool, wait. Kristina was a professional; she was probably busy with her company. She would call when she had time; Parker was sure of it.

This mattress was too soft—she felt like she was being absorbed.

She pushed herself up again and plopped down on the next one. She had a hard time trying not to imagine again what Kristina might think when she read the last line of that email. As much as it made her anxious, she was glad she'd said it. A smile turned up the corners of her lips.

She had an even harder time not remembering Kristina's words that morning outside the house... She'd never been spanked, but the dark in those eyes, the rough note in her voice, led Parker to believe they would both enjoy the experience, very much.

She steered her mind back to the task at hand. *This one is good.*

Sitting up, she bounced a few times. *Not too bouncy, but bouncy enough.*

She stood, looking down on the mattress, almost laughing at herself as she wondered if Kristina would be the one to break it in with her. *Do I want to do that at my house?*

Before she had been so worried about having Kristina in her home, making it real in that way, but somehow now, she liked the thought. A little thrill of excitement shot through her.

She had missed Kristina. She was excited to get to know her more, to continue whatever they had begun.

"Sir..." She waved over the associate. Even the slightly ridiculous price tag on the mattress couldn't ruin her good mood.

"Found the one?"

She nodded politely and followed him to the register, where she swiped her card with glee. Amanda was practically paying for this too. *God bless alimony.*

They set delivery for later that day. Stepping out into the winter sun, Parker rummaged through her purse for her cell, eager to tell Marion they were having a bonfire in her backyard this weekend. Lily was going to have to get creative to get that old bed to burn.

She unlocked her car and swiped to unlock her screen as she slid into the driver's seat. Her heart jumped. She had an email.

When she clicked the notification, butterflies spilled into her chest, because the email was from Kristina Diaz.

She opened it.

> *Parker,*
>
> *Pleased to hear you are doing well. I had wondered where you got to. Unfortunately, after such a long absence I'd assumed you had gone*

back to your wife, or changed your mind about exploring things between us any further.

I had a meeting a few days ago with a new potential partner and we agreed to move forward.

My apologies.

Kristina Diaz.

Just like that, the high Parker had found shattered. Shame burned acidic in her gut, rejection tasted like bile in her mouth.

Of course Kristina—*gorgeous, successful, amazing* Kristina—had moved on. Parker could already imagine her new partner. Young, fit, pretty—everything Parker wasn't, and the new one probably came without all the baggage that accompanied her too.

She jammed the keys into the ignition and turned on the engine, swiping roughly at the tears that had spilled onto her cheeks.

Chapter Six

"YOU'RE MOPING."

"I'm not moping!"

Parker pulled the blanket over her head and lay back on her sofa. Maybe if she ignored her best friend, she would go away. Another week had passed since the embarrassing email fiasco. Before, she had been so scared to make another bad decision. Now she was just furious with herself for taking so long to decide that she had missed her chance with Kristina completely.

"Parker Anne Freeman. Get your ass off the sofa, get up those stairs, and get your butt ready to go out!"

God, Marion was being annoying. She'd showed up fifteen minutes ago already dressed, hair beautifully curled and a bottle of vodka in her hands, triumphantly declaring they were going to ladies' night.

Parker didn't want any of it.

"It's cold outside." She sounded petulant, she knew, but she just really didn't want to do this. She didn't feel like being the oldest person in the bar tonight. Marion didn't count because she was married. "And I hate the Clam Dive. It's tacky."

Marion laughed.

"Oh no, *Amanda* hated the Clam Dive. She said it was tacky and didn't want you going there. In hindsight it was probably so you didn't end up running into her in there when she was supposed to be out of town. Now..."

The blanket was whipped off her head, and Parker stared up into the defiant dark eyes of her oldest friend.

"Up... Dressed... We're going out. If you can't do it for you, do it for me. Lily is watching Roland; I'm off starting tomorrow for two whole days in a row. I'm freaking free, and we *are* going to have a good time."

Bitter, Parker took the offered hand and let Marion pull her to her feet.

"I hate you." She grumbled as she passed Marion to head to the stairs.

"Hate you too. I'll be up in a minute with some glasses." She waved the bottle in her hand gleefully, and Parker could already feel the headache she was going to have tomorrow beginning.

"YOU NEEDED AN intervention!" Marion's voice was slightly raised so she could be heard over the music. Admittedly, Parker did feel better. One of her favorite deep-red dresses looked amazing on her, her bare arms softly shaped once again, her stomach flatter, legs more toned—even she had been surprised looking at herself in the mirror. Running and watching what she ate, taking care of herself, was finally paying off.

"I can't say I'm not glad we came." She offered Marion a grateful smile, leaning back on her stool to catch the bartender's eye and gesture for two more.

She did feel better, hair carefully styled around her shoulders, hoop earrings, eye makeup a few shades darker than she'd usually dare. The hum of liquor buzzed pleasantly through her veins. She *did* like the Clam Dive. *Fuck Amanda.*

"To new beginnings!" Marion clinked their glasses, and Parker took a healthy sip of whatever vodka cocktail they'd been drinking.

"Oh..." The mischief in her best friend's voice instantly caught her attention. "Young, tan, and gorgeous coming through the door." She watched Marion watch whoever she had spotted, not wanting to get caught staring.

"Maybe we should be looking for middle-aged, cute, and attainable?"

Marion swatted her arm, and she couldn't help but giggle. *I feel good.* Taking another long sip of her drink, she turned on her stool slightly, following Marion's line of sight.

All the alcohol in her bloodstream froze, and she snapped back to face the bar.

"Marion...that's her."

"That's the spirit! You're here, you're hot, and forty is the new twenty, and-"

Parker cut her off.

"No, M. That's Kristina."

"What?" Marion whisper-hissed, turning back to her. "That...is Miss Perfect, goddess in bed, slightly kinky but treats you with respect and you liked it?"

Parker drained her glass.

"Oh, looks like she's with someone." Her best friend's voice turned apologetic.

"That's probably the new me. The person she'd already made an arrangement with by the time I got back to her."

She was still tipsy, but somehow, it wasn't as fun anymore.

Marion ordered four shots, but Parker just wanted to leave.

"Okay. She's not seen you yet. So here's what we're going to do."

Parker closed her eyes and took a deep breath, ready to tell Marion all she wanted to do was go home and start on the ten bottles of water she knew she was going to have to down before bed to curtail a raging hangover.

"Parker, you give up too easily! She moved on, so what? Tonight you're going to drink, dance, find someone new, and make her regret passing on you for some little blonde bimbo."

"Oh my God, is the new one young?" She couldn't help but ask. Marion's face betrayed the answer.

"Less talking, more shotting."

They clinked the tiny glasses, and Parker tossed the shot back. It burned all the way down. She had barely gotten over the taste when the next was slid across the bar to her. She downed it before she could change her mind.

"Okay, they're heading this way, so get your game face on."

She panicked. Marion was smiling at her, soft and absolutely fake though to all the world it would look genuine.

"Laugh right now or I'll wave her over here."

She did, with murder in her eyes.

"She's at the other side of the bar, sweetie. She sees you."

Parker kept her eyes glued to Marion's face, afraid to look anywhere else. Marion had always been a good actress, always known how to play things in college to make sure they both got the girl.

"Oh yeah..." Marion laughed softly, looking down at her drink and then back to Parker. "She's still into you."

Something spilled into her chest. Parker didn't dare to recognize it as hope. Suddenly brave, she went to order another drink. When she turned in her seat to find the bartender, her eyes landed on Kristina's dark ones.

She looked good. Her long hair was softly curled, and the thin straps of her dress displayed her collarbones and toned arms beautifully. Earlier in the night, the prolonged eye contact might have made her blush, but with the liquor making her bold she held those dark eyes easily, finally offering her a smile before she was the one to look away.

I can do this.

"Welcome back..."

Marion bumped her shoulder, and they laughed. This time it was real.

They talked at the bar. Parker didn't even remember what the conversation had been about. Her eyes were never far from Kristina. The pool table had come free, and she had been dominating it ever since.

The woman with her was young, probably only a few years older than Kristina herself, bottle blonde, and Parker guessed she was attractive. Somehow next to Kristina she was just plain.

Everything in her stomach was knotted tight. She nodded absently along with whatever Marion was saying, her eyes caught on the bare skin of Kristina's back, exposed by the low swoop in the fabric of her dress. She still remembered her fingers pressed there.

Kristina's dark eyes flashed to her, catching her gaze, and she felt Kristina's smugness that she was watching.

"Parker..."

Kristina bent low over the table, deliberate. The hem of her dress was riding high up the back of her thighs.

"Parker."

She snapped her eyes back to Marion.

It was only when she went to reply that she realized her bottom lip had been caught between her teeth. She was sure she'd been biting it so hard there would be an indent left behind.

Marion's eyes flicked back toward the pool table and then landed on Parker's, heavy with an intent that was familiar in a way she couldn't place.

"She's watching..." Marion pushed up from her stool, slow and deliberate, and Parker's stomach rolled. "Brace yourself." The words were almost a whisper, and God this was always so weird, and it had been years since they'd done this last.

Fingers skimmed her cheeks, and her best friend stepped into her space. She closed her eyes, already knowing what was coming.

Marion's kiss was different now. It started out slower; every press of her lips was deliberate, so different than the messy passion she'd known in the six confusing months they'd mistaken friendship for love in college.

It was a well-practiced dance, a routine she half remembered, and God bless Marion, she was going for it. She shoved Marion's tongue out of her mouth with her own. As much as she knew it was meaningless, she still felt bad for LiLing. The woman was a saint, and she had put up with so much from both of them through the years.

She tried to imagine Kristina's eyes on them, imagine her jealousy, imagine that rich, dark voice. *You're mine.*

She heard Marion's breath catch as she twisted her fingers in her hair. Marion stayed close to her when they parted, studying her face, though Parker sensed the effort it was taking her not to shudder.

"You owe me..." She leaned in and kissed her one more time, soft and slow, and Parker struggled not to laugh.

"I'm going to wash my mouth out first this time, since this one was for your benefit..." she quipped.

Marion stepped away with one last long look at her, and Parker fought the urge to wipe her mouth as she watched her best friend make a beeline for the bathroom. Oddly enough, the last time they had done that was the night Marion had met LiLing.

She turned back to the bar, a smug little smile on her face, a smolder in her eyes. When they sought out Kristina, she was vindicated.

Those dark eyes were on her, burning. Kristina's knuckles were white around the pool cue, and Parker saw her swallow, hard. Even in the increasingly crowded space, for just a second, there was only the two of them in the world. *Good.*

The bartender slid another drink across the smooth surface to her with a wink, and she felt powerful, fixed, *herself* in a way she hadn't, in so long.

"Oh we got her, all right."

Marion slid down beside her and took the glass from her fingers as she lowered it from her lips. She took a long sip herself.

Parker stood from her stool.

"Going to cleanse yourself of the gross?"

She nodded. She loved Marion, but kissing her still felt how she imagined kissing your sister would.

The bar spun around her for a second as she stood. She laughed it off.

Kristina's jealous.

She moved through the bar, aware of the eyes that followed her. A woman in a booth stepped in front of her, short cropped hair and glasses, offering to buy her a drink. Her heart soared, but she politely declined.

By the time she reached the small bathroom, she was smiling. The woman who greeted her in the mirror was vibrant. Maybe it was the alcohol, but her eyes were shining, big and bright, and her blonde hair was a rich gold against her slightly flushed complexion. She filled her dress in a way she hadn't in years, and her dark lashes set off her crimson lips in a way she loved. She was back.

"Parker." The door opened, letting in the sound of the music, and she turned. Kristina stood there as it closed again behind her, dark eyes alight.

"Kristina, how are you?" Parker turned back to her reflection, fixing her already-perfect hair.

"I'm..." She paused, and Parker watched her in the mirror. "I'm glad you were able to reconcile with your wife after all."

"Oh, that's not my ex-wife."

For the first time, it felt truly good to call Amanda that. Kristina seemed to falter.

"You move quickly." She seemed to recover herself, stepping up to the mirror beside the one Parker was using. She watched her reach up to run a thumb beneath her lower lip.

"So do you. I see you brought your new...partner." Parker was careful to keep the malice out of her voice.

Kristina turned to her. Parker gripped the cool porcelain of the sink.

"My arrangement with Becca isn't going to work." Kristina's voice spilled into something dark. "And if that woman isn't your ex, would it be bold of me to assume that kiss was for my benefit?"

Parker's heart jumped in her chest. Marion would be mad at her for tipping her hand, but fuck it. She didn't want to play games; she just wanted *her*.

She took one last breath, one last glance at the woman in the mirror who, for the first time in years, she truly recognized.

She turned and her eyes met Kristina's, and she couldn't help but lick her lips at the sight of her.

"You're here, aren't you?"

Wow, my voice sounds like sex. She was about to congratulate herself on that, but Kristina spoke again.

"I don't do jealousy, sweetheart." Smugness danced in those black coffee eyes, and she stepped so close Parker's head wanted to spin.

"Really?" She studied her. Looking down at her, watching her chest rise and fall with short breaths, Parker was brave. "So her hands on me, her lips on my lips, her tongue in my mouth, doesn't bother you at all?"

Kristina's eyes were unfathomable pools. Something flashed across her face too fast for Parker to name, and then they were kissing.

Fingers in her hair tugged her head down, and Kristina's lips crashed into her own with bruising force. When a tongue skirted her lips, pushing inside her mouth, it was insistent, claiming. A hand held her hip, keeping them close, and Kristina's kiss was just as consuming as she remembered. Parker surrendered to it, lost herself in it.

When they parted, they were both breathless. Kristina's eyes flashed to the door and then back to her.

"Go into the stall, Parker."

It wasn't a request, and her heart stuttered and stopped, then raced at it. She felt brave, and bold, and *wanted*.

"Make me..."

Kristina's nostrils flared, disbelief flashed across her beautiful face, and then a hand closed around Parker's arm like a vise. Parker let herself be dragged into the stall, and pushed back against the wall, hard.

Kristina closed the door and slid the little lock into place. She paused there, back turned. The anticipation made Parker's body burn.

"Is this what you wanted?"

The words were barely above a whisper, but somehow they were loud in the quiet of the restroom. Kristina stepped toward her, predatory on five-inch heels. Impatient, Parker reached out to catch her around the back of her neck and pull her in to meet her mouth.

Hands were on her, a messiness in her touch that hadn't been there before—whether it was due to alcohol or urgency, Parker couldn't say. Fingers slid between her back and the wall, falling lower, lower, lower until Kristina was squeezing her ass, hard.

Lips attacked her mouth, trailing messily across her cheek, teeth grazing her chin, and then Kristina was feasting on her throat. Head back, eyes closed, Parker was lost and she was absolutely, gloriously found.

Kristina sucked rough over her pulse point, and Parker hummed a warning at the mark she knew was being left behind. When Kristina raised her head, there was fire in her eyes.

"Well?"

It was what Parker wanted, and she hissed her agreement as she shoved Kristina back into the opposite wall of the stall and descended on her greedily. She kissed her long, hard, thoroughly, braver now than she had ever been. She felt the stiff peaks of Kristina's nipples through the thin material of their dresses, their bodies crushed together in the small space.

Since that very first meeting their chemistry had been explosive, but here, in a dirty public bathroom, working a thigh between Kristina's, surprised when the move set a tan one between her own, Parker could barely believe her own actions. This woman was dynamite to her. She blew her wide open and set free a part of herself she'd thought was long lost.

Fingers twisted hard in her hair. The flash of pain was acceptable given the pleasure that spiked in her gut as Kristina pulled her impossibly closer, pressing her hips down into her thigh, while Parker pushed her own harder between tan legs. Kristina's breath caught. Hands squeezed her ass hard. Parker felt them working on the back of her dress, pulling it up and up and up, *and God I want it off*, hers, Kristina's, all of it.

Forgetting to be shy, she covered Kristina's breast, lathing her tongue up the side of her neck, enjoying the soft weight of it in her hands, feeling the firmness of her nipple.

The hands on her ass dragged her forward, running the length of her along Kristina's leg and grinding her own thigh into Kristina at the same time. Parker let out a shuddering breath, feeling Kristina's body flex beneath her.

Dark eyes found her own; then fingers were around her throat, and she was falling backward. The hard expanse of the wall caught her, Kristina's other hand behind her head, saving it from impact.

Kristina didn't waste a second. As soon as they were moved she was reaching up to kiss her again, Parker's dress hiked obscenely around her waist, taunting fingers running too soft over the wet material of her underwear.

Parker let out a whine.

"Isn't this what you wanted?"

She didn't answer the question, leaning down to kiss her. The hands in her hair turned to a vise, holding her back.

"I want to watch you, baby…"

Heat exploded in her chest. The hand between her legs cupped her, giving her just enough pressure to be absolutely maddening.

"That's right…" Kristina's eyes were dancing, triumphant, hungry. "You're mine."

Am I?

"What about your brand-new sub?"

Parker hadn't meant to say the words, but they spilled out anyway, breathless.

A beat passed, and then the change in Kristina was immediate. The fingers in her hair went loose, the hand between her legs fell away, and Parker wanted to scream, to cry, to beg. *Why do I ruin everything?*

"You're right."

She watched Kristina run a hand through her hair, cursing.

"I need to end things with her first."

God, she has morals? Parker knew she should be pleased, but holy crap, she just wanted to finish what they had started, what her body was coiled tight, hot, wet, *aching* for.

"I'm sorry, sweetheart. I owe it to her to do the right thing and end things respectfully."

Kristina's bottom lip was between her teeth, and Parker leaned back against the wall, unashamed. Kristina's gaze ascended her bare legs slowly, lingering on her exposed panties at their apex for a few long seconds. Kristina grit her teeth.

"Pull down your dress."

Parker did, grudgingly.

"Can I pick you up tomorrow, maybe at noon? We can get lunch and talk." Kristina swallowed hard, hungry eyes searching Parker's face as she continued, "Maybe finish what we started here?"

Parker didn't want to wait, but what choice did she have? Drunk as she was, she wanted her, now.

"Fine."

She was pleased with herself for the iciness in her tone.

Kristina nodded, smoothing her hair and straightening her dress.

"I'll see you tomorrow then."

She moved to the door. Her fingers lingered on the lock. Parker's heart beat hard as she hoped, stupidly, desperately, selfishly, that Kristina would give up whatever moral high ground she was trying to maintain and just turn around and fuck her like they both clearly wanted.

"May I kiss you good night?"

She had not been expecting that. Kristina's shoulders were stiff, the words careful.

"That depends on what you plan on doing afterwards?"

Kristina crossed the space back to her, trapping her against the wall. "I plan on taking Becca home safely and ending our arrangement respectfully."

Parker wanted so much to be mad at her. Kristina's dark eyes roamed her face. Her tongue darted out to wet full lips as her voice dropped low, rougher.

"And then I plan on going home and trying not to keep myself up all night thinking about you, Parker, while I wait to see you again tomorrow."

The words hit her low in the gut, the thought of Kristina...*keeping herself up*...was sweet, sweet torture, as ridiculously keyed up as she already was. Kristina was studying her face, and Parker knew she was waiting. The question came again, softer.

"May I kiss you, sweetheart?"

Damn this woman. Parker swallowed hard. The intensity that had lived between them since their very first meeting was thick in the air now, and the need for her was like a physical ache. She had tasted the upper hand, and a little part of her enjoyed pushing Kristina's buttons, playing with her.

She imagined Kristina wasn't used to asking permission for anything. She paused, giving herself a moment to remember this, then took great joy in granting it.

"You may."

Chapter Seven

THE SUN WAS high in the sky when the sleek black car pulled up to the curb. Parker struggled up from her doorstep, squinting in the bright light even behind her large, dark glasses.

"Morning, sunshine."

Kristina looked fine, fresh even, and Parker hated her just a little bit.

"Why are you wearing workout clothes?" Parker asked.

She slid down into the seat, dumping her purse. Her morning run had been forgone in favor of an extra three hours in bed, and too much aspirin.

"Just finished yoga."

God, she was not ready for those images... *Kristina does yoga.*

"Here, drink this."

A metal travel cup was thrust into her hands. Parker eyed her over the console.

"If this is any kind of liquor, I'm going to puke in your fancy car. You know that, right?"

Kristina laughed, and somehow, the sound alone made her feel a little better.

"Just trust me. Try it."

She took a healthy pull on the straw, scrunching up her face while she swallowed.

"Veggie juice?"

"Fruits, veggies, a few secret ingredients... Drink it all and you'll be as good as new in half an hour."

The liquid sloshed against the back of the cup as they pulled away from the curb too fast—how was she going to survive Kristina's driving?

Grudgingly, she took another long swallow, holding her breath and drinking as much as she could, because really, what did she have to lose?

"You do yoga?"

The wind whipped Parker's hair back, and the breeze actually felt nice on her face. Leaning back against the headrest, she continued to suck on the straw, watching Kristina, soaking up her presence again after being denied for so long.

"I do. Maybe I'll show you some time."

Kristina winked, and caught somewhere between wanting to purge her stomach and wanting to kiss her, Parker closed her eyes and tried to breathe.

"Where are we going?"

"I thought we could go back to my place..."

"Oh no, no..." She glanced at her across the console. "We need to talk, like actual words, somewhere public."

"Are you saying you can't control yourself around me in private, Professor?"

Kristina made a scandalized face. All Parker could think was that she was beautiful. She seemed more open now, somehow obtainable in a way she hadn't been before.

Parker drained the last of the mystery juice, glad to be done with it.

"I'm saying we should talk first."

They took a hard left into an IHOP, of all places.

"Like you wanted to talk last night?"

God, she was still too fuzzy right now to keep up with Kristina, who was clearly in fine form.

"You're so full of it this morning, Miss Diaz." She shot the words back. This new playfulness between them made something in her chest flip. "I demand you cut me some slack, at least until I've had breakfast."

Kristina hopped out of the car while Parker was still fumbling with her seat belt. When she looked up, the door was being held open, and dark eyes were shining down at her.

"As you wish."

Parker followed her into the restaurant, eyes lingering on her backside. *Yoga pants are wonderful.*

Kristina stopped at a booth, gesturing politely for her to sit. Parker slid onto the bench, surprised when Kristina sat down beside her instead of across the table. She slipped off her sunglasses and studied the menu, agreeing that water was fine when the server came by.

This was surreal somehow. Just twenty-four hours ago she was moping on her sofa; now she was here, slightly hungover in IHOP, with Kristina.

"So, last night..."

Kristina's hand settled high up her thigh, and her body snapped to attention under the touch.

"What about it?"

Parker glanced sideways, tucking her hair back behind her ear, noticing Kristina watching her.

"I'm glad I ran into you."

How did she get so intense, so fast?

A beat passed between them. Parker's lips got hot under Kristina's gaze. She licked them without thinking. The fingers on her thigh flexed.

She couldn't think straight around her. She cleared her throat.

"Did you get your...friend home okay?"

She needed some distance; she needed to eat and feel a little more human and get through some of the questions she had for Kristina, before she let herself be tugged back under her spell. This time, she needed to do things right.

She wanted this. Somewhere between losing it all, and finding Kristina again, she had become sure of that much at least. She just wished she had a little better idea of exactly what *this* was.

"Yes." The hand fell away. "Are you still upset that I left?"

Parker shrugged, turning her eyes back to her menu.

"You didn't leave me with anything I couldn't take care of myself."

It was true. She had touched herself last night, at home in her new bed, her body still aching from their time together in the bathroom.

Kristina's breath caught audibly. *Good.*

"Are you ladies ready to order?"

Parker smirked to herself at the irritation in Kristina's voice as she ordered some obnoxious-sounding smoothie and two buttermilk pancakes. Parker took her time, ordering bacon pancakes and a coffee, hoping the grease would soak up the last of the hangover and leave her free to enjoy the afternoon with the woman.

When the server strode away, Kristina reached into her purse and produced a small stack of paper.

"Standard NDAs. We both sign, so we're both protected. Take all the time you need to read it, but it basically says we both agree not to disclose what we do together in private or the nature of our relationship to anyone outside it."

Suddenly they were back to all business, any trace of levity gone from her voice.

Parker thumbed through the pages. Was this just standard procedure for Kristina? She hated the thought, an unpleasant reminder that she was one of many, the next in a probably long line of subs.

"And what exactly will be the nature of our relationship?"

She kept her eyes on the printed lines, though she wasn't really absorbing the words.

"Domination and submission, sex, mutual pleasure..."

Kristina's eyes were on her, but she didn't look up.

"So we just meet for sex? We don't...talk or go out to eat or...date?"

"I don't do dating, sweetheart."

The reply sounded rehearsed.

"Like you don't do jealousy?"

When she glanced up Kristina was frozen, her mouth twisted into a grim line as she watched her.

Parker signed the NDA with a flourish.

"Parker...I'm not looking for a relationship. I like to interact in a very particular way in bed, and in my private life. We have great chemistry, and I believe we're compatible in that respect, but beyond that..."

She sounded...*scared?*

"We can talk, and of course we'll build a connection. Submission is about trust, and I'd like to earn yours. I'd also like to give you a good spanking for your attitude last night, but I need to know you understand. I just don't date, period."

Kristina was beautiful, even with her hair pulled back, her makeup lighter than Parker ever remembered seeing it. She had an effortless sort of beauty, the kind that shone even under the harsh restaurant lights.

Parker wondered briefly how she had become this. How someone so young, and clearly bright, so full of potential, had arrived at the point where the only kind of personal relationship they wanted was based around power play.

"I just got out of a fourteen-year marriage. I'm not looking for a relationship right now." The words felt like a half-truth to her, but she swallowed the feeling down.

"But eventually, you will be, and then our time together will end. You'll move on to your happily ever after, and I'll move on to my next sub."

The thought of Kristina with someone else dug under her skin more than it should.

"Like the girl who was with you last night?"

Parker rearranged her cutlery, not looking at Kristina, trying to process the casualness of all this, the fact it was temporary. Kristina had filled a void for her. Even in her absence, missing her had somehow replaced her previous feeling of not being in control of her life. The thought of removing her from her world entirely was...uncomfortable.

"Now who's jealous?"

She didn't dignify that with a response.

"We have something to offer each other right now. Our arrangement stands until either of us decides that's no longer the case."

Parker nodded. Her headache started to fade, though she still felt foggy, deflated by the conversation.

"Until then, you're mine."

Her head snapped up at that, though Kristina was busy smiling up at the server who was setting down their food.

Parker cut into her pancakes, letting the joy of grease and carbs in her mouth smother the tension still hanging between them. She was aware of Kristina watching her, but they ate in silence.

Kristina pushed her pancakes around her plate, taking a few bites, then set them aside. She settled for sipping her smoothie. Parker watched one hand, with perfectly manicured nails, disappear deliberately under the table. It landed so high on Parker's bare thigh that it made her jump, her cutlery scraping her plate.

"So…" Heat was already building embarrassingly in her stomach. The pads of Kristina's fingers pressed between her thighs even though she squeezed them tight, and a flush crept up Parker's neck.

"Tell me more about your company? You said you're involved in logistics?"

She needed to think about something, *anything*, other than the fingers pressing, pushing, closer to her underwear.

"What do you want to know about it?"

Kristina's smile was lazy, and she looked relaxed, totally at ease with the fact that she was working Parker's dress up her legs in the middle of a family restaurant.

"Logistics is a pretty broad term… What do you, um… ship?"

Kristina's fingers pressed against the seam of her panties, and she instantly hated her past self for choosing those stupid, sexy, skimpy little lace ones. The texture of the lace over her increasingly sensitive flesh was torture. She looked up. Kristina's lip was between her teeth. The sight sent another flash of arousal right down to the spot where she was touching her, and Parker had to look away.

The fingers wiggled, rubbing against her. She almost dropped her fork, but she needed something to do, anything, to distract her from what Kristina was doing.

Has she scooted closer? Parker felt trapped, Kristina on one side keeping her in the booth, the wall on the other.

"The safe word is 'red.' You remember that?"

Parker nodded, hacking at her pancakes some more though her appetite had long vanished, replaced by a hunger of an entirely different kind.

"Good girl."

We're doing this...here, now... Kristina was so calm, so put together, and so completely in her element. Parker's heart raced, and she was surprised to find this was thrilling to her as much as it was mortifying.

"Now, you don't give a shit about my company right now, do you?"

She shook her head, cheeks burning, eyes on her plate.

The fingers between her legs stilled.

"No what?"

She felt her heartbeat in her throat.

"No, Mistress."

It was a whisper. *God, what if the server comes back?*

"Open your legs for me, now."

She inched her thighs apart, the pleather of the bench sticking horribly to her skin. Kristina laughed, rich and dark, and the sound made Parker's heart skip.

"Wider."

Parker's breath was coming hard, and she didn't dare to look up, to look around, too scared of what she might see, of what the rest of the restaurant might see on her face. She parted her legs just a fraction more. Her body jerked when her panties were pulled to the side.

"Do you like this, Parker?"

She had to close her eyes when a finger slid over her soaking flesh, her body already betraying her answer.

"Yes... Mistress..." Her answer was breathless, the cutlery digging into her palms painfully in her vise grip.

A finger bumped against her clit and her body jumped.

"Look at me."

The fingers in her panties were rubbing her softly, and she was biting the inside of her mouth, hard. She wanted to throw her head back, close her eyes, and give in, yet the presence of the few other patrons, the staff in the restaurant, kept her on edge, alert, ashamed, and excited.

When she looked up, Kristina was watching her hungrily. The temperature between them felt nuclear, and she risked a glance around, convinced someone, somewhere must have noticed. It seemed nobody had.

"Put down your knife and fork."

Her hands shook as she placed them on the table and moved instead to grip its edge. Her nipples strained against the soft silk of her bra. Wetness soaked her tiny panties, the inside of her thighs.

"Eyes on me, sweetheart." Kristina licked her lips, long and slow, and Parker wished for her to kiss her.

"Do you want to come, right here, like this? Dress hiked up, legs open for me in the middle of this restaurant?"

Yes, no... Her mind warred. The fingers between her legs rubbed her harder, and she whined softly. She was caught, not permitted to look away, and the hunger in Kristina's dark eyes was undoing her. She was embarrassed, mortified at herself that she was getting off on this, yet it was so good. She was already closing in on the release she'd craved for weeks in Kristina's absence. She didn't have it in her to ask Kristina to stop.

"I don't know..." Tears pricked the back of her eyes, too many feelings, too much to process, trapped as she was between pleasure and desire and her own sense of propriety, of shame.

"Soon you won't have to worry about what people think; the answer will be easy for you. If it pleases me then yes, because you'll trust me enough to know what pleases me is always for your pleasure too."

Kristina's hand slipped away from her, and Parker swallowed a whine, eyes back on the tabletop as wet fingers slid down the inside of her thigh, leaving a slick trail in their wake.

"Now, take off your panties and put them in my hand."

Her eyes shot up to Kristina's face and then down to her hand, open, waiting on the bench between them.

"Right now, sweetheart. Discreetly."

With her heart beating in her throat, Parker began the process of wiggling out of them, lifting her hips slightly and working them down her legs through the fabric of her dress. Her cheeks burned crimson as she disappeared under the table, taking a deep breath in the dark, hardly able to believe her own actions as she bent and tugged the material from around her ankles and pressed it onto Kristina's waiting hand.

When she emerged, their server was smiling down at her.

Adrenaline shot again into her blood, and she offered her a watery smile in return as Kristina handed over her card, seemingly unfazed.

Parker walked to the car behind the younger woman, trying to keep her gait natural while pressing together her thighs, her excitement from earlier coating them messily.

"So you never told me what happened when you disappeared for two weeks?"

Kristina pressed a button and the car roared to life. They were back to normal conversation, acting like Kristina hadn't just shoved her damp panties into her purse, like Parker wasn't sitting there, tugging down her dress and feeling utterly exposed and completely naughty without them.

"When you dropped me off, my ex-wife was in my house having sex with the woman she cheated on me for years with, in my bed."

Somehow, still caught in the haze of what they'd been doing, Parker found it was easier simply to lay out the facts.

Kristina's reaction was the mildest she'd experienced from anyone after telling them that particular news.

"And how did that make you feel?"

Really?

"Honestly... Angry, used, like it wasn't enough that she cheated on me the whole time but she had to come back and rub it in my face. Not good enough I guess..."

"And why's that?"

They were weaving in and out of traffic, and all this was strange, the wind whipping her hair, her arousal drying sticky between her legs while they discussed Amanda.

"I don't know."

Kristina just nodded.

They didn't speak again until they pulled up to the curb at Parker's house, only this time, Kristina pulled the car into her driveway.

"Are you coming in?"

Her heart jumped at the thought.

"If it's okay with you."

Parker nodded shyly, holding down the hem of her dress with one hand as she struggled to get out of the car without exposing herself. When she looked back, Kristina was still in the driver's seat, laughing.

Parker stormed to the front door. She opened it and tossed her purse and keys on the side table, waiting for Kristina to join her.

"So just...make yourself at home. Do you want something to drink or...?"

Kristina stepped close to her, and the mood shifted in a breath.

"I want you to show me where your bedroom is."

Dutifully, she led the way up the stairs.

Chapter Eight

"IS THIS THE offending bed?" Kristina strode right past her, into her bedroom, and immediately made herself at home on the edge of the mattress. Parker hovered awkwardly in the doorway.

"No, actually, it's in the backyard—well, what's left of it... We sort of had a bonfire."

Kristina laughed, amusement creasing the skin around her eyes before her expression turned serious again.

"Come in and close the door."

Parker's stomach flipped. She did, acutely aware of the eyes on her.

"Take off your dress for me."

"I, um..." She glanced around the room, unsure what she was looking for. It was broad daylight, the curtains were open, and Kristina was staring at her, expectant. When did she become this person who was ashamed of her body?

Eyes on the floor, she shrugged out of her jacket and grabbed the hem of her dress and tugged it over her head in one quick move. She let both garments fall to the floor, crossing her arms at her hips, wishing she at least still had her panties.

She heard Kristina get up from the bed and pad across the carpet toward her.

"Parker... Look at me."

Shame burned hot in her gut as she lifted her head.

"You are a beautiful woman."

A hand reached for her waist, the pads of Kristina's fingers tracing its curve.

"Yet that's how you undress yourself for me? You hide your body?"

Parker swallowed hard, an apology on her lips, though she kept them tight closed. Surprisingly, Kristina leaned forward and kissed her. Her lips were soft at first, and when her tongue parted Parker's, it pushed deep into her mouth. Slowly, her shyness fell away, desire taking over.

"You are so fucking beautiful." Kristina took a step back. "When I ask you to undress for me, sweetheart, I want you to remember that."

Parker watched, mesmerized, as Kristina trailed her tan fingers up over a flat stomach, across the fabric of her tank top, skirting the hem of her jacket until she pushed it back off her slim shoulders.

"That's right, baby, watch me..."

Kristina was so confident, so sure. She was hypnotic, and Parker knew she couldn't look away, even if she wanted to. Kristina slid her hands down her body, over the swell of her breasts, down the curve of her waist, and God, she was flawless. Anticipation tickled Parker's stomach as that skintight tank was inched up, softly toned abs revealed, before it was pulled over her head.

She was breathing hard as Kristina worked her fingers into the waistband of yoga pants—*she's killing me in freaking yoga pants*—and then those pants were falling down smooth thighs and Kristina was looking at her, standing in her bedroom in just her matching black underwear. Parker's stomach flipped.

"Like what you see?"

She nodded, quickly remembering herself. "Yes, Mistress."

Somewhere during the display her hands had fallen away from covering her, resting at her sides, fingers balled into fists. Kristina reached up to let down her dark hair and shook it out around her shoulders.

"I don't want you ashamed and hiding. Do you understand?"

Kristina reached up and unclasped her bra and let it fall off her arms and tumble to the floor with the rest of her clothes. Her nipples were already hard. Parker licked her lips at the sight.

"Yes, Mistress."

Kristina stood there, naked except for her panties, watching her. The charge between them was dizzying.

"Take off your bra."

Parker swallowed hard. Her hands shook at her sides and she willed them to still, steeling herself.

Slowly, carefully, she ran the pads of her fingers up the outside of her thighs, over the curve of her waist, closing her eyes and trying to let herself feel the touch.

"That's right, baby..."

Kristina had taken a step closer, she knew without opening her eyes. She let her hands trail forward, up over her flat stomach, feeling the weight of her own breasts in her hands.

"Good girl. Now look at me..."

I don't know if I can do this with my eyes open. She did it anyway. Kristina was watching her intently, and rather than feeling embarrassed, somehow, she felt wanted, desired, desirable.

"Take it off for me."

She reached behind herself slowly and fumbled with the clasp a little before, finally, it sprung free and she slid the material slowly down her arms.

Kristina was shameless in studying her breasts, and her nipples hardened under the attention, everything in her aching to be touched.

"Good girl."

Rather than stepping forward, Kristina stepped to the side, gesturing to the bed.

"Shoes off and lay down."

Parker kicked off her sandals and moved to comply, trying to hold on to that feeling of being pretty, sexy, desirable, though she felt exposed all over again laid out on the bed, naked. The mattress dipped as Kristina sat beside her.

"Touch your breasts."

Her cheeks flamed. Kristina swung her legs up onto the bed and lay down beside her. She leaned up on an elbow to watch.

Parker reached up, her heart beating wild, hands shaking as they settled over her breasts. Her nipples strained under her palms, already stiff, sensitive.

"Show me how you like to be touched, sweetheart..."

Sadly, she didn't even know anymore. She tugged a little on the twin peaks, letting out a satisfied exhale at the heat the action shot between her legs.

"Touch your body..."

Kristina raked a single finger down between the valley of Parker's breasts, circling her navel before sliding it away. Parker shuddered at the touch. Her hands followed its path, feeling the goose bumps it had left in its wake, across her skin.

"That's right…" Kristina's dark hair fell over her shoulder. Parker felt her cool breath on her throat.

"Spread your legs, baby…"

Parker swallowed hard, raising her hands back to her breasts, closing her eyes, trying to lose herself in the sensation, to distract herself from the embarrassment of being laid open before her.

"Now show me how you touched yourself last night."

Panic and arousal shot in her chest, spilling into her blood, thrilling.

"Did you lie right here, thinking about me, Parker?"

She nodded, and Kristina leaned down to kiss her, rough and messy.

"Were you imagining me fucking you in that bathroom stall?"

"Yes, Mistress…" She grit out the words, breathy, rough, as she dipped her fingers between her legs to find she was once again wet, hot, completely wanting for Kristina.

She rubbed herself slow and steady, resisting the urge to go rougher, harder, and just explode. She wanted Kristina to be the one to make her come. The thought alone made her clench.

Dark hair tickled her chest as Kristina lowered her head and sucked a nipple between her lips. Parker keened and then hissed as she felt the rough graze of teeth followed by the hot lathe of a tongue.

Kristina let it go with a pop.

"Do you masturbate with toys?"

The question shocked her, but she swallowed hard and answered, rubbing herself just a little faster, determined to stay in the moment.

"No, Mistress."

"Do you fuck yourself?"

The question confused her. She looked up into dark eyes, curious, blushing.

"Do you put your fingers inside yourself, Parker?"

Her hand stilled for a minute as she stumbled over the answer.

"Keep going."

The order was immediate and she complied.

"I...not usually..."

Is that weird?

Kristina's fingers closed around one of her nipples and rolled it softly. Her eyes fell shut. It felt so good to have Kristina touching her.

"When was the last time someone was inside you?"

God, what's with all the questions? Honestly...she didn't know. Things with Amanda had been pretty mechanical, a means to an end. She'd usually just rubbed Parker until she came and then rolled out of bed to shower.

"I'm not sure."

Kristina sucked in a breath.

Pressure was building between Parker's legs, and it saved her from being horribly embarrassed over all this.

"Do you want me inside you, sweetheart? My fingers, my tongue...maybe my toys."

Her hips bucked shamefully at the words.

"Yes, Mistress."

With a laugh, dark and breathy, Kristina tugged her hand away from herself and guided it up to her mouth. Parker watched, torn between frustration at the loss of stimulation and fascination, as her own pale fingers disappeared between plump lips.

She couldn't help the soft hum of approval, arousal, that spilled from between her closed lips as teeth and tongue attacked her fingers. Kristina made a show of tasting her on them, and Parker watched, greedy.

"Keep your hands up here."

Her wrists were raised above her head, and she grabbed her headboard obediently. Her breath caught as Kristina climbed on top of her, slipping a thigh between her open ones, settling over her.

When lips covered her own and a tongue pushed into her mouth, she tasted herself.

"I'm going to fuck you now, baby..."

God, yes.

A hand covered her, and she parted her legs, eager.

"That's right, sweetheart. You're all mine."

Kristina kissed her roughly, moving to bite and suck gently at her neck.

"This is all mine."

Kristina rubbed her before her fingers slid lower, teasing. Parker's hips bucked up off the bed.

"Tell me you want it..."

Kristina's lips were so close to her ear... Kissing, nipping, sucking. Parker moaned. *I don't want it—I need it.*

"I...want it, please..."

A finger pressed against her entrance, and she whined.

"Be specific."

This was mortifying, and hot, and *screw it.*

"I want you inside me, please."

A hand tangled in her hair and pulled her head back on the pillows, leaving Parker's gaze locked on Kristina's as the heel of her hand pressed hard over her clit, and one finger sunk into her.

She clenched, heard her own moan, long and low and pornographic, but she couldn't think, couldn't see anything except those dark eyes drinking it all in.

When was the last time someone fucked her, wanted her, made her feel good like this?

"So hot…" Kristina was looking down at her with such reverence, such hunger, that it was impossible not to believe her. Parker's hips jumped without her permission, pushing the finger deeper inside. She gasped at the feeling.

Kristina laughed, leaning down to kiss her.

"I want to feel you come on my fingers…"

She was so…explicit, and somehow the words only made Parker hotter. She ran her hands down Kristina's back, all soft skin and smooth muscle, following the curve of her spine, feeling the shape of her ass, squeezing hard when the finger inside her began to move.

"Hands up. You feel so good, Parker…"

She moaned at the words, her body already winding hot, tight.

When the finger that was pushing her closer slipped out of her, she couldn't help but whine. A hand tugged her hair, rough.

"So impatient, baby…"

Kristina was looking down at her again, eyes wild, hair mussed, and it was so obvious from her face that she loved this.

The width of two fingers pressed at Parker's entrance, and she licked her lips, nervous.

"Do you trust me?"

She nodded, and Kristina eased into her, and yes, she felt so full, so fucked. She couldn't help her hissed approval.

The heel of Kristina's hand grinding against her, the curl of her fingers inside her, they were pushing her closer to the edge. She tightened on them.

"Are you going to come for me, sweetheart?"

She nodded, panting out the words. "Yes, Mistress..."

She was so close.

"You don't come without permission. Do you understand?"

Fingers thrust rough into her with the question, and her walls fluttered. She tensed her thighs quickly to try to stave off her impending orgasm.

"Yes... Mistress..."

Crap, I'm so close.

"I'm... Can I come, please?"

Those fingers were fucking her, urgent now, deep and unforgiving, and she was clenched so painfully tight on them, leaving them rubbing against the most sensitive parts of her. Sweat ran down from her hairline. She was going to finish soon, whether she had permission or not.

"Please, Mistress..."

She moaned out the words, her walls clenching hard, dangerous.

"Come for me, Parker."

She exploded. Her hips had been working higher and higher off the bed. They crashed back to the mattress with staggering force, and then she was limp, shaking, falling apart with Kristina's fingers still working deep inside her.

The noises she made were pornographic to her own ears, but she couldn't bring herself to care. She felt so full, so used, so fucking good. Kristina still pumped her slowly, even as her orgasm ended. A thumb brushed her clit, and Parker's body began to tighten again.

"I... God..."

This was so unfamiliar to her. She didn't think she'd ever had an orgasm like the one she'd just enjoyed. Her legs were almost numb from being clamped so tight together, yet she recognized the build of another, forming deep in her stomach.

"I..."

Her body jumped, and her wetness spilled onto Kristina's hand.

"You're mine, Parker..." Kristina panted the words above her. "Mine to use, mine to pleasure."

Her legs were shaking.

"Relax for me, sweetheart."

Parker was torn between relief and sheer frustration when the fingers slipped from inside her. Her hips jumped off the bed when she felt the press of Kristina's fingers back against her entrance, a third one joining them.

"Relax."

It wasn't a request. Kristina's mouth covered hers, pushing her tongue rough inside, her thumb working over her clit while slowly, torturously, wonderfully, she eased three fingers inside Parker.

"Good girl." The praise came with a swift kiss on her mouth, and Parker's head was spinning.

Legs spread, laid out naked, three fingers in her, she was here, in her bedroom, with Kristina, about to have another mind-blowing orgasm.

"Come on, baby." The fingers inside her twisted, stretching her deliciously, and she let her head fall back. Kristina's nipples were hard against her own, heat building between their bodies. Her legs were shaking and she was aching, exhausted, yet her body was coiling tight again, quivering around Kristina's skilled fingers.

"You're so fucking beautiful like this..." Three sharp thrusts accompanied the words, and Parker moaned long and loud. Everything in her clenched tight. Kristina leaned down and kissed the shell of her ear, rubbing her thumb hard over Parker's clit as she increased the pace of the digits inside her.

"Tell me you're mine."

She could hardly draw in a breath to say the words, but somehow, she managed it.

"I'm...yours..."

The fingers inside her pushed impossibly deeper.

"Good girl, now come for me."

Her body obeyed immediately.

Finally, when she was totally spent, Kristina slipped out of her and rolled to lay beside her. When Parker held her breath and swallowed, trying to regain control of her body, she heard Kristina's unsteady breaths in the silence.

Between her legs was a mess, but more than anything, she wanted to touch Kristina, to make her feel as good as Parker felt after all that. She pushed up onto a shaky elbow.

"Can I touch you?"

She reached out and settled a hand just below Kristina's breast, tentative.

"You already are."

Dark eyes burned up at her.

"I want to touch you like you touched me."

The confession embarrassed her, but she forced herself to hold those eyes. Kristina swallowed.

"Go ahead."

Parker was suddenly shy, Kristina laid out beside her, naked save for the thin scrap of black silk that was her panties.

Letting still-shaking fingers glide higher, she covered Kristina's breast and squeezed gently. She saw the echo of the action in Kristina's eyes. This woman beguiled her. She was so young, yet she filled the role of authority, power effortlessly, and Parker found that she bowed to her easily, willingly.

"May I take these off, Mistress?"

She trailed her fingers down to trace the waistband of her underwear. Kristina was beautiful, hair splayed on her pillow. Parker burned the image into her mind, the want, the flash of uncertainty in those dark eyes she fought so hard to hide.

"You may."

She pushed up to her knees and dragged the panties down Kristina's legs, forcing her eyes not to linger at the apex of Kristina's thighs, clean shaven. Tossing the material aside, Parker swung a leg over Kristina's hips. Firm hands came up to hold her own, as she settled herself over Kristina, her still-sensitive flesh meeting Kristina's stomach, making her shudder.

Kristina purred beneath her.

Parker leaned down and kissed her, pushing her tongue into her mouth, enjoying the semblance of control she was being allowed.

She moved her lips down to Kristina's neck, across her collarbones, scooting down her body to take a stiff nipple into her mouth. She sucked hard and Kristina twisted rough fingers in her hair.

"Get on with it, sweetheart."

Looking up at Kristina through thick lashes, she nipped at the stiff flesh, just a hint of defiance, before obediently, she slid lower. She kissed her way over firm abs, feeling the muscles tense below the skin, over one hipbone and then the other. Her eyes landed on a web of scars, pale against otherwise tan skin, taut over Kristina's left hip. She reached up to touch them, wondering what had left such a strange series of marks there.

"Now..."

Kristina's voice was low, rough from above her, and Parker pressed a quick kiss to the lines before dipping lower, kissing below her navel and scooting down between her legs.

"Are you sure you want..."

She nipped the inside of a tan thigh, guiding Kristina's legs apart.

"Yes, Mistress... I want to."

The muscles in Kristina's stomach jumped as Parker's breath caught her between the legs. Parker smirked. The fingers in her hair pulled tight.

"Put your mouth to better use before you end up over my knee."

With one last smile, Parker dipped her head. Kristina's fell back on her pillow as Parker ran her tongue over her.

Kristina was quiet during sex. Though her body jumped and jerked, her thighs tightening in a way that told Parker she was doing good work, she barely made a sound. Parker ran her hands up smooth thighs, sucking her hard, letting her tongue sink down lower, testing. Her reward was a soft gasp, and she smiled against her.

"Do you like that, Mistress?"

Parker nipped the soft skin on the inside of her thigh, enjoying the way her body jumped in response. Kristina was gorgeous, all tan skin and super toned. *God bless yoga.*

"Yes."

The words was almost a hiss, the fingers in her hair pressing her head back down, impatient. She kissed Kristina and then popped back up.

"May I use my fingers on you too?"

Parker dug the pads of them into the inside of Kristina's thigh and slid them higher, eager.

"No."

The response surprised her.

"Pleasure me with your mouth, sweetheart. Quickly."

Parker lowered her head. Kristina's breathing grew heavier above her, and she worked her over hard, sucking, licking, nipping, eager to draw any kind of sound from her. She was close, her body was tight, *and fuck it.*

Parker sucked hard on her clit and moved lower, circling her entrance once before she thrust her tongue inside. A soft sound from above was her reward. Kristina's insides quivered pleasingly, before she pulled her tongue away. Kristina growled.

Back to licking and sucking at her clit, innocent, Parker ignored the sound. When the hips below her began to rock slightly, she pushed her tongue into her again. This time a longer, lower, rougher moan rewarded her, followed by a whine when she pulled it away.

"So help me, Parker..."

She fought not to laugh, lapping at her, ignoring the hands that were tight in her hair.

"Do you need something, Mistress?" She let her lips graze messy, wet over Kristina's flesh as she asked, teasing.

One minute she was licking Kristina; the next Kristina was sitting up, strong hands wrapped around Parker's biceps, pulling her up and pushing her back, laying her on the bed. Before she had time to process, Kristina was crawling on top of her, tugging her hands up.

"Lace your hands behind your head, now."

She did, licking her lips as Kristina moved upward, knees settling on either side of her shoulders. Her stomach clenched as she realized what was happening.

"You are mine to use. Do you understand?"

She nodded. Rough fingers closed around her cheeks, squeezing.

"Words."

"Yes, Mistress." They came out horribly distorted with Kristina holding her face, squishing her lips together, before she let her go.

"Now open your mouth."

She did, eyes locked on Kristina's as she lowered herself down onto her. This was so much hotter than she imagined it would be. Maybe that was just because of Kristina, who was shamelessly riding her face, hands covering her breasts, eyes on Parker's.

Kristina hummed her approval, and something inside Parker came alive at the sound. She reached up, taking hold of Kristina's slim hips, holding her still, while rather than just letting her move, she started to lick her, suck her, fuck her again, ignoring the growled warning from above.

When Kristina's hips bucked and her thighs started to shake, Parker shoved her tongue inside, giving up on breathing, eager to see Kristina come. Kristina pitched forward with a long, low moan Parker knew she would be hearing in her dreams for weeks.

Her body shook, and her fingers fisted the pillow beside Parker's head. Parker lapped her obediently until finally, spent, she scooted away.

Kristina rolled off her, breathless, and Parker reached up to wipe her mouth, triumphant. Something had changed between them in the time they were apart. If they had been compatible before, they were explosive together now, and she couldn't help but be proud of the fact.

"What are you smirking at?"

The words were rough, lazy. Parker turned her head, the smug smirk on her lips turning into a genuine smile at the sight of Kristina, laid back on her pillows, eyes heavy-lidded, looking utterly sated, and absolutely beautiful.

This was good.

Chapter Nine

HER PHONE BUZZED against her leg inside her purse, and suddenly, it was difficult to pay attention to what the head of the department was saying. She nodded along, making the right faces, agreeing and sighing in the right places, but her mind was on Kristina.

She was still sore from the weekend, and somehow, she still wanted more. Finally able to say her polite goodbye, she turned to head back to her office, pulling her phone out of her purse. She swiped the screen, eager.

What are you wearing today, Professor? This meeting is utterly boring, help a girl out?

She'd had a feeling they were heading toward this. Since the weekend they had exchanged more texts than Parker thought she had ever sent anyone, and it was kind of thrilling.

Kristina was always flirty, always intense, but she was also sort of sweet, and when she asked Parker how her day had gone, Parker felt like she actually wanted to hear the answer.

She closed the door, pleased she had another thirty minutes before her office hours started. Parker sat back in her chair and let herself indulge.

Black slacks, gray silk blouse, black pumps with a four-inch heel, leather jacket. You?

It had been so long since she had done anything like this, she was suddenly unsure. *Are we sexting?* Not knowing what else to do, she pressed Send.

She had barely finished taking the rubber band off her first stack of assignments to review when her phone buzzed, loud against her desk in the quiet.

> *I'm not asking because I'm thinking of starting a clothing catalog, sweetheart. Describe it to me in a way that makes me imagine taking it off you.*

Her heart bumped. She swallowed, feeling like an idiot as she looked down her body, shy despite herself. Taking a deep breath, she let her fingers move over the screen.

> *The slacks cling in all the right places, the material is soft and smooth against the inside of my thighs and feels nice through my panties, thin black lace that sit low on my hips.*

She licked her lips, her body stirring. She was doing this, here, at work. She was torn between feeling naughty in a good way, and a bad one.

> *The blouse is thin silk, so thin that anyone who came by right now would see my nipples getting hard from typing this for you.*

She pressed Send before she could change her mind, equal parts eager and nervous for the reply. It came almost instantly.

> *Good girl. Are you alone?*

She hadn't even put down her phone.

> *Yes.*

Her cell buzzed again, two pictures arriving in quick succession. One of Kristina, gorgeous in a fitted gray pinstripe business suit, the other with the same outfit, suit jacket gone, blouse open, toned abs and deep-maroon bra visible, her dark eyes burning. Parker's body roared in response. Both pictures were clearly taken in a bathroom mirror.

Shouldn't you be in your meeting?

She pressed her thighs together. She still had fifteen minutes before office hours began.

The correct response is "thank you, Mistress," sweetheart.

A smirk twisted at her lips.

Thank you, sweetheart.

The more she pushed Kristina's buttons, the more she found she liked her reaction, and the more she caught herself fantasizing about Kristina finally making good on all the threats to take her over her knee. The thought turned her on more than she would admit.

Oh Miss Freeman, I do hope you like pink. That's the color your backside is going to be the next time I see you.

Heat was building low in Parker's stomach, and she was turned on now to the point it was uncomfortable. She should stop, go to the bathroom, and splash some water on her face, clean herself up, and get ready for office hours, yet it was so hard. Kristina, this thing they were doing, it was addicting, it gratified her and left her high, every time.

Then I look forward to our next meeting, Miss Diaz.

She tasted the younger woman's frustration in her one word reply.

Friday.

Four days was too long to wait. Her phone buzzed again.

I'd like to see some of these professor outfits for myself. How do you feel about me paying you a visit at work sometime?

Her heart thumped, and she knew she was setting herself up for a whole new kind of delicious torture with her answer. If she started imagining Kristina could turn up at any moment, she would drive herself mad.

I wouldn't mind you visiting, as long as we keep things PG-13 on campus.

Begrudgingly she eyed the clock and typed out another message.

Office hours start in five, have to go. Talk later?

Her heart was still racing as she walked to the bathroom, feeling utterly filthy as she exchanged smiles with the students waiting outside her room for her to return. In the stall she hurriedly cleaned herself up, rushing to wash her hands. Before she could leave, she caught sight of herself in the mirror.

Her eyes were shining, cheeks flushed. She looked happy, so happy it was disarming.

Her phone buzzed in her pocket, and she pulled it out, addicted.

Talk later, sweetheart.

IT WAS ONLY Wednesday. Marion and LiLing had left Roland with her while they had date night, Marion being off tomorrow thanks to her weird hours at the lab. Parker loved taking care of her godson, and she was glad her best friend was getting some quality time with her wife, but she had been dreading seeing Marion all day.

Since signing the NDA she had no real idea what she could or couldn't share. Naturally Marion was chomping at the bit for information, and Parker knew she could only put off giving her something so many ways, unless she just came out and told her she'd signed a legal document that possibly prevented her from sharing anything more than she already had about Kristina.

The woman herself had been at a business dinner all night, and with her phone quiet, Parker had found she had far too much time to think. She was eager to see Kristina again on Friday, and even more eager to open the package that had been sitting on her doorstep when she arrived home. Neatly written in the corner was *Sender: K. Diaz.* A text message earlier in the day had informed her she would receive mail and not to open it until she was told.

The sofa was soft underneath her. Roland was asleep upstairs in the guest bedroom. The antiquated baby monitor she still used for her own sanity sat on the coffee table.

It was like Kristina had awakened something inside her that night at the club, the following day upstairs in her room, and ever since it had been insatiable. As her mind wandered, she thought about it all: the text messages, the way Kristina's breath had caught in her throat, the soft moan that had spilled from her lips when Parker pleased her. Parker remembered the press of fingers inside her, the tug of a hand in her hair, and again, she was aching.

The thought of touching herself with Roland in the house seemed dirty, wrong, but she was horribly tempted. Her fingers skirted the smooth fabric of her pajamas, and she tuned out the TV, remembering how her name sounded in Kristina's mouth, the way she'd...

Her cell buzzed on the coffee table, making her jump, guilty. She grabbed it.

> *Bathroom break. Some of these people are insane. How's your night going?*

She tapped out a reply, pleased Kristina had thought to message her.

> *Good. Roland's in bed. Just lying on the sofa debating my morals of late.*

The reply was instant.

> *Explain?*

She sighed.

> *Just feeling guilty about how often I want to...indulge myself since I met you.*

The phone rang. Swallowing hard, excitement spilling into her stomach, she accepted Kristina's call. She heard the swell of a crowded room around her; then the line went suddenly quiet.

"What type of indulgence are we talking about?"

Her voice was already low, rough. Parker's body reacted to it immediately.

"Well hello to you too."

She heard Kristina sucking her lip.

"I don't have time for your sass right now, Parker. Why do you feel guilty about pleasuring yourself?"

Her cheeks burned at the question.

"I, um... Aren't you at a party?"

"I stepped outside and it's freezing."

Oh. That explained the curtness.

"I don't know. I just think it's not...right to want to do it so much, especially when you have a child asleep in the house."

Kristina snorted.

"Sweetheart, pleasuring yourself, taking care of your needs, is an important part of self-care. There's nothing not right, or unnatural about it."

She sounded so sure Parker almost wanted to believe her, but she wasn't sure Kristina Dominatrix Diaz had an entirely accurate worldview.

"I'm not sure polite society would agree."

"Who exactly is polite society? Old white men who want to believe a woman exists solely for their pleasure and God forbid she get any of her own, especially without their input."

Wow, she was passionate about this.

"I want to hear you say this, Parker."

Kristina paused, and even over the phone, Parker felt herself falling under her spell.

"It's okay to enjoy sex. I deserve sexual gratification."

She swallowed hard and then repeated the words back to her, forcing herself to feel them.

"Good girl. Now as much as you've made my night hell, thinking about you at home doing that while I have to entertain these idiots, I do have to get back. Did you open the package?"

Parker tried to keep her exhale quiet, disappointed Kristina was about to disappear again.

"No, Mistress." The words were soft, breathy against the phone.

"Good girl. I want you to touch yourself until you come tonight, and I want you to think of those words while you do, okay?"

She hadn't expected that. She swallowed hard.

"Yes, Mistress."

She held her breath, waiting for Kristina to hang up the phone. Though she was excited by the command, her heart was oddly heavy at saying goodbye. There was a long pause.

"I miss you too, sweetheart."

The line went dead.

SHE'D DONE AS Kristina asked, twice. Even going as far as sending her a picture of herself laid there on the sofa, cheeks flushed, eyes still dark from her last orgasm. She hadn't received a reply.

Marion had texted asking if they could pick Roland up in the morning, and she'd agreed. Sometime afterwards she must have fallen asleep. She woke up on the sofa to the sound of the doorbell, her back aching.

Shit.

She scrambled to her feet. She smoothed down her hair, socks skidding on the hardwood of her hallway right as Marion and LiLing stepped through the front door.

Marion laughed.

"He still asleep?"

Parker nodded, disoriented.

"What time is it?"

"Almost six. We wanted to get him out of your hair before you had to start getting ready for work."

She mumbled her thanks, already leading them through to the kitchen. She smashed the button on the coffee maker, bidding it to work quickly.

"What's this?"

Crap.

The package from Kristina was in Marion's hands, and she was turning it over with interest.

"It's nothing."

LiLing was looking over her shoulder at it.

"Nothing from K. Diaz. Isn't your girlfriend's name Katie..."

"Kristina," Marion supplied unhelpfully, eyes shining with glee. Parker groaned.

"She's not my girlfriend, and it's some sort of surprise. I'm not allowed to open it yet."

LiLing seemed satisfied with that, but Marion's eyes held her own with interest, and it was just too early for all this.

"Not allowed?"

Parker nodded, feeling her cheeks flame.

"What happens if you open it anyway? Will she *punish* you?"

"Oh my God... I'm going to wake our son." LiLing disappeared up the stairs.

Mercifully, the machine beeped, and Parker was able to busy herself with pouring a cup of coffee, turning away from Marion who she knew now was like a dog with a bone.

"Come on, P. You've been so secretive lately..." Her voice turned soft. "Did something happen? Is it not going well?"

Part of her wanted to say yes just to get her best friend to leave the subject alone, but she was a horrible liar, especially when it came to Marion.

"It's going good, great actually." She took a long swallow of coffee. It burned all the way down. "Kristina is just sort of private, and I'm trying to respect that."

She could feel Marion tugging conclusions from her words.

"You like her."

She crossed the room to her best friend, snatched back her package, and replaced it with the mug in her hands.

"Of course I like her. I'm sleeping with her, aren't I?"

Marion sipped from her mug, studying her over the rim.

"No, it's more than that. You *like her*, like her."

"Oh my God, are we twelve?"

Do I?

"Ready to go?"

LiLing appeared in the doorway, a sleepy Roland clinging to one of her legs. Parker took back her drink and followed them through the house. She hugged them as they stepped out into the cool morning air.

"Don't get attached, sweetie."

Parker watched them leave down her driveway, a cute little family of three, something that wasn't ever going to be in her future.

Of course she wasn't going to get attached to Kristina. She just filled the void, for now.

THEY'D SPOKEN BRIEFLY last night, but watching her second to last Friday class file out, Parker caught herself again looking forward to seeing Kristina tonight.

Between that and wondering what was in the package she'd been instructed to take with her today, Parker was being driven mad. They had no solid plans for the weekend yet, but Kristina had said they would meet today, and Parker hoped beyond hope that was still going to be the case.

She grabbed her cup, eager to get a refill before she had to give her final lecture of the week, when the buzz of her cell stopped her. It was a text from Kristina.

> *Go to the bathroom and open your package, then call me.*

Excitement shot in her chest, and she grabbed her purse, coffee long forgotten as she hurried to the single-stall bathroom down the hall. Inside, she tore into the paper, nervous and excited. The stupid brown box had been taunting her for the better part of two days now.

The little silver balls inside confused her. After a quick Google search of the brand on the card, they excited her. With the shiny spheres in her palm, she dialed Kristina.

"Kristina Diaz."

She mustn't have looked at the caller ID.

"Hi..."

"Sweetheart..."

The change in her tone made Parker smile; it was softer for her, and that gratified her somehow. The line on Kristina's end was noisy, a swell of voices in the background.

"Do you like your gift?"

Parker was glad she'd looked up what exactly it was before she made this call.

"Well, they're not what I expected, but I'm excited to try them out. Tonight?" she asked, hopeful.

"No." The edge to Kristina's voice already told her something was about to happen. "Now. I want you to put them inside yourself then go and give your last lecture. If you're uncomfortable with the idea, you can veto with the safe word, but I find the thought of them inside you for the rest of the day very hot."

The last two words were pure sex. Was she okay with this?

"I... Can I try them out first?"

They were just balls. How bad could it be?

"Of course. You might want to put them in your mouth first."

The jump lost her, and Kristina must have realized it from her silence.

"It makes them warm and wet, sweetheart. I love how oblivious you are sometimes."

Parker wanted to tell her to shut up but thought better of it.

"And are you just going to be on the phone while I do this?" *In the bathroom, at work,* her mind finished unhelpfully.

The line muffled for a second, and she could barely make out Kristina asking someone for directions before she was back.

"No, I actually have to go. Think you can handle things from here?"

Parker nodded, clacking the little balls together in her palm. *They're sort of cute.*

"Yes, Mistress."

Feeling brave, she ended the call. A text came almost immediately.

Let me know if you decided to wear them.

The time on her cell told her she had ten minutes. *God, I'm actually doing this.* She lubricated the balls like Kristina had suggested, feeling dirty as she unbuttoned her slacks and maneuvered one, then the other inside herself. *Thank God they're small.*

Pleased with herself, she adjusted her clothes and shot Kristina a quick text.

> *I did.*

They really weren't bad at all. She felt full, naughty because she knew they were there, but beyond that they weren't much of anything. Was she disappointed?

Gathering her stuff, she took a step toward the door and almost fell down. The balls bumped together inside her, the little weights inside them rolling around, making them almost hum. *Damn Kristina.*

Collecting herself, she unlocked the door and started down the corridor, trying to ignore the pleasant thrum of the balls inside her that seemed to be getting worse the further she walked. Thank God she could sit down and give her lecture.

> *You're evil.*

She shot off the text as she passed her room, aware her face was becoming increasingly flushed as she strode in the direction of the auditorium.

A tech was already setting her slides up on the screen, and students were just beginning to fill the stands. She thanked a god she didn't believe in when she could finally sit down.

> *I try.*

Now they had woken her body up, it was like Parker couldn't forget the presence of the stupid balls. She forced herself to take a deep breath, ignoring the pressure between her legs.

It was almost five minutes past three, and the hall was half-full, probably as good as she was going to get.

She nodded for the tech to lower the lights, and grudgingly stood to introduce herself. Her phone buzzed just as she did.

Did I tell you you're beautiful today?

Adrenaline shot white-hot into her stomach. When she looked up from her cell all she could see was the glow of screens, outlines of faces, eyes on her, expectant.

Was Kristina here? Of course not. She was being stupid.

"Good afternoon, everyone." Her voice was rough, and she cleared her throat. "For those of you who don't know, I'm Professor Parker Freeman from the English Lit Department, and today we're going to be discussing common tropes in nineteenth-century novels."

THE LECTURE WAS hell. Even sitting down she was all too aware of the balls inside her, rubbing her, reacting to every shift of her weight, leaving her crossing and uncrossing her legs uncomfortably. Though she knew it was illogical, a part of her was still on edge, still wondering what that last text had meant. Was Kristina just being sweet? How did she know how she looked today? Was she out there somewhere?

Parker nodded to the tech, feeling like she'd run a marathon, glad the hour had come to an end. The rustling of papers and bags and coats was already rising in the stands in front of her. She combed them quickly, half-relieved, half-disappointed when her eyes didn't find Kristina.

"I will make these slides available online for those of you who want them. Any questions, please email myself or one of my TAs."

Just the thought of standing up to pack her bag was terrible. She took her thumb drive back from the tech with a smile and wished him a good weekend, then lingered over stacking her notes neatly and clipping them together. When the room had emptied some, she picked up her phone.

Is there a reason for the flattery? Also, the last hour was hell. I stick to my earlier conclusions, you're evil. Does it get you off knowing I spent the last hour horribly turned on?

Screw it. She felt brave after...that.

She stood, shoving her papers into her bag, calculating in her head where the closest bathroom was so she could take the damn things out. Her phone buzzed, and she almost didn't pick it up to look.

It's not flattery if it's the truth. And to answer your question, yes, it does get me off, but what gets me off even more is seeing it.

Her head snapped up. What the hell was Kristina talking about?

Her eyes combed the seats, row after rapidly emptying row, yet still, she didn't see Kristina. Her heart was beating hard, and she was way too keyed up. She stabbed out a reply, irritated.

What are you talking about?

No reply came. Frustrated, she gathered her bag and shrugged her jacket back on, trying to ignore the roll of the balls inside her as she stood.

"Excuse me, Professor. I have a question."

She clenched tight on the balls, the feeling stealing her breath. She would know that voice anywhere.

"Kristina..."

Her name sounded rough, breathless, and mirth danced in those dark eyes in response. She stepped up onto the podium, and Parker's heart flipped at the sight of her.

She was gorgeous in casual clothes, jeans, and a band tee. She could easily pass for one of Parker's students. Was it crazy that she wanted to kiss her about as much as she wanted to have her bend her over the desk and make all the torture of the last hour worth it?

"Hey, beautiful."

Kristina's eyes were on her, hunger mixed with something she couldn't recognize inside them. Remembering where they were, Parker glanced around. Only a few students remained, and even they were in the process of leaving.

"What are you doing here?"

She hated the catch in her voice, how something in her chest flipped as Kristina stepped closer to her. She watched purple-painted fingernails run along the edge of the desk... How did the action make her hotter?

"I told you, as much as I enjoy the thought of that, I enjoyed watching it with my own eyes much, much more."

When Kristina's eyes rose to meet her own, their connection was electric. She was a second away from losing it, from surging forward and kissing her.

"Professor Freeman?"

Parker's eyes snapped in the direction of the interruption, everything in her crashing back to Earth when she came face to face with the Dean striding toward them.

"Dean Thomas." Her voice shook. "How are you?"

His response was polite and then he was in front of them on the podium, and Parker's brain seemed to have exited the building. The three of them were left in a moment of awkward silence, all caught under the weight of the introduction that was dying to happen.

"I uh, Dean Thomas, this is my...um..."

Kinky sex partner?

Kristina stepped forward to save her.

"Kristina Diaz. Parker is my partner. I'm here to pick her up."

One hand was held out to the dean while the other settled on the small of Parker's back, soft and possessive in a way Parker knew she would have absolutely loathed from Amanda, but loved from Kristina.

The dean's eyebrows flew toward his hairline. *He probably thinks she's too young or too...*

"Diaz. As in Logistica?"

Kristina nodded, and then the two of them were off, talking business—apparently the dean knew her father. Parker just tried to smile politely, watching the interaction and wishing she could forget about the balls inside her, and somehow recover from the shock of Kristina being here, and then the dean being here, in dizzyingly quick succession.

"Professor."

She snapped back to attention. A smile still lingered on the dean's face, and of course Kristina had charmed him too.

"I just wanted to make sure you'd be attending the benefit next month for the new library wing. I think it's important the staff, especially in the Culture and Languages departments, show their support, if possible."

She nodded politely.

"Of course, sir. I wouldn't miss it."

Kristina was watching her. The skin on the side of her neck prickled at the feeling.

"Excellent, well, it was lovely to meet you, Miss Diaz. Tell Mario I said hello, and you ladies enjoy your weekend."

Parker smiled politely as he shook Kristina's hand again.

The minute the door swung closed, Kristina stepped into her space, picking up her purse and bookbag, leaning so close Parker could feel the heat of her body against her side.

"May I carry these for you, Professor?"

Parker took a shuddering breath.

"That depends. May I go to the bathroom and remove these...things, before we walk to the car?"

Kristina laughed against her ear, soft and breathy. It sent goose bumps across her arms.

"No, sweetheart, absolutely not."

Chapter Ten

PARKER BREATHED A sigh of relief when they pulled up in front of Kristina's house, though the feeling didn't last long. Her car was older, bigger than Kristina's little speed machine, and she honestly had no idea it could move so fast until she made the mistake of letting Kristina drive it.

"You seem tense?"

The question was lazy as they headed through the door into the house.

"Did you take an Uber just so you could talk me into letting you drive my car?"

The balls rolled inside her, and Parker grit her teeth. She was caught somewhere between turned on and annoyed, the adrenaline of the car ride still filtering its way out of her blood.

"No, I took an Uber because I thought driving two cars back here was pointless. Are you mad at me?"

Kristina had produced a bottle of wine. She paused with the corkscrew halfway to its top. She looked concerned.

"No, I'm not. I'm just…"

Frustrated, turned on, riled up.

The bottle was set on the counter with a thud.

"What's the issue?"

Kristina crossed the distance between them, and Parker licked her lips. The shift in the mood was palpable. Of course Kristina already knew. She had planned this, all of it.

Forcing her face to relax into an expression somewhere close to contrite, Parker tried being sweet.

"May I please take out the balls now, Mistress?"

Kristina cocked her head.

"No. What else?"

Parker tightened her jaw. She was tired of being teased without anything really happening. Being uncomfortable, well, *it sucked*.

"Stop scowling and tell me what the problem is, Parker. Now."

Kristina's voice rung with an authority she had never heard. Something dark flashed in her eyes, and Parker's heart raced in response.

"I want you to fuck me."

The words poured out of her and her cheeks burned, but she held Kristina's gaze, defiant.

"Really?"

Kristina shrugged out of her jacket, and Parker's body stirred at the action.

"And do you think that's the best way to get what you want? Being grouchy, and asking me in that way?"

Crap.

She shook her head.

"Words." It was a hiss.

"No, Mistress."

"No."

Kristina repeated her answer. She took her hand and led her through to the living room.

"Do you remember what I said we were going to do the next time we met?"

I do. Parker licked her lips.

"Yes, Mistress."

"The safe word is 'red.' Do you understand?"

She repeated her agreement.

Kristina sat back on the sofa, expression unreadable. The energy in the room set Parker's teeth on edge; it was dark, darker than anything she had ever experienced with Kristina. Was this what punishment would be like?

"Come here."

Her heart jumped. Suddenly she missed playful Kristina, gentle Kristina, Kristina who called her "sweetheart" and opened the door for her. The thought of getting spanked had been so hot to her, but now it was apparently happening, she wasn't so sure.

She crossed the room and sat beside her. Vaguely aware her hands were shaking, she clasped them in her lap.

"I'm not mad at you. Do you understand?"

Kristina liked this; she could see it on her face. Parker nodded.

"You're in control, Parker." Kristina leaned forward, and kissed her softly. When she pulled away, Parker chased her lips, rewarded with another kiss, longer, deeper, a tongue running slick over her lips before it pulled away. "Say the word and we stop."

"Yes, Mistress." Her mouth was suddenly dry.

Kristina unbuttoned her pants, and slid down the zipper. Anticipation already had her breathing hard.

"Relax, baby."

Fingers closed tight around her wrist, and then she was tugged forward and sideways until she landed across Kristina's lap, her hair falling around her face like a golden curtain. A leg settled over her thighs, a hand between her shoulder blades keeping her in place, and she was absolutely humiliated. It only got worse when her pants and underwear were tugged down, leaving her backside and the tops of her thighs exposed.

The word "red" was on the tip of her tongue. The room was silent, and she was mortified, everything inside her screaming that this was horrible, embarrassing, degrading. She squeezed her eyes closed and tried to listen to Kristina's already-short breaths. Never had she experienced anything like this.

She jumped when fingers touched her, rubbing over her uncomfortably wet flesh, moving the balls inside her. *It feels…good?*

"I'm going to spank you, Parker, because you talked back to me, and gave me attitude on multiple occasions. Do you understand me?"

Parker sucked in a breath, lost between the pleasure of the balls rolling and clacking, humming inside her, and the shame of this whole thing.

"Yes, Mistress."

Fingers brushed her clit and her body jumped.

"You don't have to count, but I'm going to spank you seven times, and I expect you to lie still for me. Understand?"

She agreed again, everything in her tense, waiting for the first blow to land. Instead, those fingers just continued to tease her, touching her and rubbing her, pressing against her entrance from behind in a way that made her want to roll her hips back and take them inside. She forced herself to hold still.

Kristina's fingers were moving over her easily, growing slick with her desire. Parker was just starting to relax when the hand was pulled away and the first blow landed, stinging across her left butt cheek. She cried out, the sound distorted when Kristina cupped her hard, and the burn across her skin mixed with the pleasure of the pressure of the balls inside.

She wished Kristina would say something, anything to pull her back from the strange place she was hurtling toward, so many emotions crashing over her, her body so sensitive, overstimulated but wanting.

Another slap landed, this time lower, the edge of fingers catching her between the legs wetly, jolting the balls inside.

They came in quick succession from there, three more, across her left cheek, her right, and then almost between her legs completely. Kristina rubbed her, touched her, and she was embarrassed and confused. Somehow, she was close to coming from this.

The sixth one was hard. She grit her teeth, but a soft sound of surprise still spilled from between them. Damp fingers soothed the burn for a second before they were back between her legs, rubbing her clit, teasing her entrance. Parker was torn between wanting to get away from her and just wanting to get fucked by her.

The last blow landed right against her sensitive flesh. Her body quivered in response, and she jerked on reflex when a finger pushed into her. A growl from above made her still, the muscles in her stomach jumping as the balls were fished out. A tear fell onto the hardwood below, and she watched it, surprised, a tiny puddle on the dark oak.

"Good girl... My good girl."

Relief washed over her at the sound of Kristina's voice. It was familiar, *my Kristina*, it was rich and warm, and she heard Kristina's arousal inside it.

"You did so well."

Two fingers were pushed into her, and she hissed at the burn. Somehow she felt tighter after the balls, everything in her overstimulated, almost sore in her need. Kristina's thumb brushed her clit, and Parker jumped as teeth nipped her stinging bottom gently.

"Do you want to come?"

I don't know. Fingers twisted in her and it became clearer. She needed some sort of release. Tears were collecting on the floor below. She was ashamed and she was somehow freed.

"Yes, Mistress, make me come, please..."

She had a strange urge to tell Kristina she was hers. The headspace she was slipping into scared her, and she pressed her lips together tight.

She focused instead on the fingers fucking her, the thumb on her clit, the heavy breathing that was growing faster above her, and then she was coming. Her orgasm arrived out of nowhere, touching every part of her, winding her horribly, uncomfortably tight, and then leaving her completely slack, spent, and crying.

She was somehow pulled up and turned over. Sitting in Kristina's lap, held to her chest. Parker let her face get lost in the dark hair at the crook of her neck, confused and embarrassed by her reaction. Her body was still shuddering with the aftershocks.

"You did so good, sweetheart..." That voice washed over her, arms were holding her tight, stroking her back, her hair, and she felt horribly vulnerable and scarily safe. *Why is this splitting me open?*

Kristina held her for a long time, their quiet breaths the only sound in the otherwise silent house. The sun had almost disappeared totally behind the horizon when finally Kristina jostled her. Parker felt stupid. She was forty years old and clinging to this woman half her age like a lifeline.

"Are you okay? The first time can be intense."

Right... She was just another on a long conveyor belt of subs for Kristina. Everything that was so profound and new to her was probably just another check mark on the *Dominants-R-Us* standard issue bucket list.

Parker pushed up to a shaky stand and stepped away, struggling to tug her pants back up over her burning behind.

"Parker..." Kristina's voice was careful, guarded.

"It was fine, Kristina. I know this is all routine for you, and you've probably done this a hundred times before. I just need a minute to catch up."

Her voice was taut, bitter, but it was too late to hide it. Kristina caught her arm when she tried to walk away.

"If you think you aren't special to me..." She paused, a disbelieving little laugh kissing her lips. "Then you're crazy."

Parker turned to look at Kristina, and dark eyes held her own. Swallowing down her fears, Parker leaned down and kissed her. It was careful, gentle, passionate in a way that made the inside of her chest feel warm.

When they pulled apart, Kristina looked shaken.

"How am I special?" The question was quiet, and she asked it even though everything inside her was screaming for her to shut the hell up and just continue the moment between them. For the first time, she felt she was experiencing whatever Kristina was underneath all of her dominant walls.

Kristina's tongue darted out to lick full lips, and Parker brushed a strand of dark hair back over her shoulder, a little guilty that she was making her uncomfortable.

"If you were anyone else I'd either give you some cream for your behind, or apply it myself, then send you home."

The thought of leaving her now hurt in a way Parker didn't understand.

"Do you want me to go?"

Kristina shook her head. She swallowed hard, and when she spoke again, her words were a whisper.

"No... I... I want to take you to my room and undress you, take a shower with you, and then rub arnica on your backside." A sliver of her usual confidence emerged with the comment, and Parker blushed.

"Then you can please me if you like, or I can pleasure you some more. Either way, I'd like to take care of you for a little while longer before I let you go."

As messed up as it was, Parker's heart soared at the words.

"Okay."

THE SENSATION OF being watched woke her. Amber light was just beginning to break the darkness, and she guessed it was a little before dawn. They must have fallen asleep in bed after their shower. Her butt still smarted where it met the covers.

"Hey."

The dark eyes that had been watching her turned wide, caught.

Still half-asleep, too tired to process or second-guess, Parker rolled into her. The length of Kristina's naked body pressed against her own was bliss, and she luxuriated in it.

"Why are you awake?"

Kristina stumbled over the answer, and it was adorable and Parker was too sleepy to think much of it. She leaned down and kissed the words off Kristina's lips, threading her fingers through thick dark hair, holding her close.

Even after the erotic confusion of the spanking, her body sparked, though the reaction was slower, gentler, deeper than usual.

Soft hands held her hips, trailing up her sides, running lightly down her back. She wanted Kristina to touch her everywhere, just as much as she wanted to feel her fall apart in her hands. Their tongues danced soft, and she slipped her thigh between tan ones, pleased when it was met with the slide of hot, wet flesh. Kristina felt so good, so warm and smooth against her. Somehow they just fit together like this, in a way that pleased Parker's sleep-addled brain tremendously.

She hummed her contentment, pressing one last soft kiss to the corner of her lips before she trailed kisses lower. She was working down the side of her neck when Kristina tensed beneath her and pulled away. Parker groaned.

"I...actually, I have yoga!" Kristina seemed awfully surprised by her own appointment. Unpleasantly awake now, Parker squinted through the dark, confused, as she watched Kristina hurry around the room, grabbing clothes and bumping into the dresser, which sounded painful, before she scurried out of the door.

What just happened?

WEARING YESTERDAY'S SLACKS, and a clean T-shirt she had found on the dresser in Kristina's room, she stepped tentatively out onto the beach.

Parker had watched Kristina through the big glass window in the bedroom for longer than she would admit. She enjoyed the way her body twisted easily into the various poses, found her fascinating as she flexed deeper into them as the sun rose behind her.

She was just as beautiful now, knees tugged up to her chest, sitting on her yoga mat in a hoodie and sweatpants, watching the sun rise over the sea.

"I brought you coffee."

Parker held out the mug, hoping it would smooth things over, give her a reason for being out there, a reason to get past whatever had caused Kristina to run that morning. In hindsight she thought she knew, but she wasn't ready to think about it.

"Thanks, sweetheart. Join me in my office?"

Parker passed the coffee down to her and rolled her eyes, sitting carefully beside her on the mat.

"Quite the view you have out here."

She studied the horizon, blue and red and gold as far as she could see.

"Yeah, it is..." A note in Kristina's voice made her turn, and when she did, Kristina was looking at her, something stormy in her eyes. If Parker was braver, bolder, stupider, she would have kissed her.

Kristina looked away and the moment broke.

"I have business meetings today, starting at eleven."

Parker nodded, embarrassed, aware that she was being asked to leave.

"Right. I'll go and um, grab my stuff. I just wanted to bring you coffee and..."

She didn't know what else to say, already scrambling to her feet. Kristina's strong fingers caught her around the arm.

For a moment, she thought Kristina was going to say something profound; then the expression in her eyes changed, and she seemed to think better of it.

"Can I see you out?"

Parker nodded, reaching down a hand, laughing as she tugged the shorter woman to her feet, both of them spilling their coffee, though neither of them seemed to mind.

By the time she was in her car, Parker felt better, Kristina leaning down through the open window watching her turn the keys. Something had changed between them, she knew they both felt it, and somehow, it left them off balance, out of sync again when they had just found their rhythm together.

"I really do have meetings all day."

She looked up at Kristina, suddenly shy.

"I know." *Is my disappointment at leaving that obvious?*

"If I can get through enough today, maybe I'll have some time tomorrow. I'll call you?"

She nodded.

"Drive safe, sweetheart."

Parker was disappointed when Kristina pushed off the side of the car and stood back in the driveway to watch her leave. She'd wanted her to kiss her.

Chapter Eleven

"I DON'T REALLY know where to start, so I'm just going to come out and say it."

Parker nodded, squeezing Marion's hands tight in her own, trying her best to be present and here and engaged with whatever huge thing had her best friend looking so nervous, and kind of excited.

Things with Kristina had been fraught. She hadn't been able to meet on Sunday, and now almost a whole week later, sitting on Marion's sofa on Friday night, Parker worried she had messed things up between them permanently.

Marion's fingers returned her squeeze.

"We're having another baby."

"*What*?" Her reaction was as loud inside her head as it was outside of it. When had they decided this? How had she missed it? *God...am I really that wrapped up in my own crap?*

"That's...amazing, that's so amazing! When did you guys start thinking about this?"

Marion looked guilty.

"You've had a rough year, P-bear. I imagine the last thing you want to hear about is our boring back and forth over baby number two."

The words burned, as well intentioned and careful as they had been. Parker heard the true meaning. Her best friend hadn't wanted to burden her with yet another reminder of all the things she had that would never exist in Parker's own messed-up life.

She swallowed down the hurt.

"So how are you going to...I mean you're thirty-nine."

There were tears in Marion's chocolate eyes as she nodded.

"I know. We weren't sure it would take, but we contacted Roland's donor again and it took three tries but..."

Parker gasped, surged forward to hug her, and then released her chokehold, suddenly conscious of the new little life between them.

She pulled back and held Marion's face between her hands, searching her eyes.

"I am so ridiculously, wonderfully, happy for you. You know that, right?"

Tears spilled onto her fingers, and Marion sniffled and nodded.

Parker tugged her into a hug, swallowing the tears in her throat. When they pulled apart, LiLing was in the doorway, a bottle of sparkling grape juice in one hand and three champagne flutes in the other.

"I take it she's told you you're going to be a godmom and an auntie again?"

Parker nodded, genuinely overcome with love and happiness, and so much gratitude for these wonderful, strong women who had become her family.

"I can hardly wait!"

She crossed the room and pulled LiLing into a hug.

Marion (best friend from the bar) and her wife told me last night they're expecting another baby, another godson/daughter/niece/nephew for me.

She wasn't sure why she sent the text to Kristina. She hadn't gotten a reply from her since Thursday, but lying in bed on Saturday morning, she realized she had nobody else aside from her brother to share the news with. The buzz of her phone surprised her.

Congratulations.

Her heart fell. She was tired of waiting, and wondering. If Kristina didn't want to see her anymore, she wished she would just say so. Running a hand through her hair, she tapped out a message.

Do you want to end our arrangement?

The tears in her throat as she pressed Send surprised her. She tossed her phone onto the mattress and closed her eyes, telling herself she'd done the right thing. *It's better just to know.*

The harsh buzz of her cell cut into her worrying, and she picked it up, surprised to see Kristina on the caller ID. *Oh God, is she going to do it over the phone?* Was this part of her code about ending things respectfully?

She declined the call. A text came almost immediately.

Answer me, right now, sweetheart. If you're unable please step outside and take the call. It's important.

The phone started to ring again, and panic spilled hot into her chest. Taking a deep breath, she swiped to accept the call, and lifted it to her ear.

"Parker?"

She swallowed.

"Kristina... Hi..."

She sounded flat, fake.

"What on earth makes you think I want to end things with you?"

Hope shot through her, dangerous.

"I wasn't sure. You've just been so distant lately and I thought—"

"Hold on, baby."

Kristina cut her off, and Parker tried to ignore how her heart raced at the endearment. She'd only ever called her that while they were doing *stuff*.

Parker could hear her down the line, muffled as she discussed something in clipped, hurried tones. She sounded far away, and Parker imagined she was holding her cell down while she spoke.

"I need five minutes, Frank. Close the door and tell Janelle to hold my calls..."

She's at work? Parker tugged the phone away from her ear briefly. *At ten thirty on a Saturday morning?*

"Parker?"

"I'm here."

She studied her ceiling and waited, suddenly unsure what to say. The silence down the line was deafening. Finally, Kristina spoke.

"Of course I don't want to end things. I apologize if you got that impression. I just..." She sighed. "Usually when things get this way with the company, I put whatever arrangement I currently have on hold, sort of like a time out. The other person can see someone else if they want, and once I have more free time we touch base and decide if we'll resume, or move on."

Parker swallowed hard.

"Maybe I should have done that here, but I didn't want that with you... So I wasn't really sure what to do, and then work was insane..."

She was smiling like an idiot, because Kristina didn't want to take a break, and she was also apparently an idiot, and a clueless one when it came to personal relationships beyond arrangements and kink.

"Kristina, you could have just talked to me."

She could practically hear the gears turning in Kristina's head.

"I texted you that work had been busy?"

"Right, but that one-line text, and calling me to explain work is really insane and you're probably going to be pretty unavailable for the next week are sort of different things."

Kristina swallowed audibly.

"That's...probably true. Do I need to apologize? I probably should... I am sorry, sweetheart."

It was so hard not to be disarmed by her like this, so uncertain when she was usually so sure.

"That's okay."

And somehow, it was.

"Please don't think I don't want to continue our arrangement. That's never been the case. It was the opposite actually."

Parker smiled at that.

"Think I could steal you at some point this weekend, just for a little while?"

The pause on the other end of the line didn't bode well.

"I'll make it well worth your while, Mistress."

The soft growl her words elicited was the sweetest reward for her boldness.

"God, I've missed you and your attitude, Miss Freeman."

She was smiling, a grin splitting her face for the first time in a week.

"I missed you too, Kristina."

She heard a male voice on the other end of the line, and wished desperately for an answer before Kristina hung up.

"I'll try and get done early tonight. I'll text you, okay?"

She nodded, correcting herself quickly when she remembered Kristina couldn't see her.

"Okay…"

The line went dead, and she was left clutching her phone to her ear, a stupid smile on her face.

KRISTINA HADN'T TEXTED. Parker had tried not to be too disappointed with that development. Her day had been better, her grading and planning passing easier, now she knew Kristina was just honestly, genuinely busy, though she had really hoped to see her.

The TV flickered, and she was hardly watching, close to drifting off when her phone buzzed on her nightstand.

Still awake?

At least Kristina had bothered to message like she'd said, even if it was only going to be to say good night.

Barely.

She was falling asleep again, waiting for a reply, when a loud knock on her front door jolted her awake. Her eyes flicked to the clock. Almost midnight. She lay still; hopefully whoever it was would just go away. She was pretty used to being home alone. Even when she was married she was in the house by herself for the majority of the time, yet when the knocking came again, she was a little spooked.

She grabbed her phone and typed out a quick message.

Someone's knocking on my door...

She wasn't sure what Kristina could do from her house, but it made her feel better that someone knew.

I know.

The text didn't make sense.

It's cold, are you going to let me in?

Her panic dissolved into glee. She threw off the covers and rushed down the hall, patting down her hair, grimacing at her flannel pajama pants and tank top—there was nothing that could be done for it now.

Without bothering to check the peephole, she slid back the dead bolt and opened the door, a smile already breaking over her face when she saw Kristina on the other side.

"Hey, beautiful."

She looked so tired. Parker reached out and tugged her inside. She closed the door behind her and locked it, forgetting to be self-conscious as the cold night air made her nipples strain against the thin material of her tank.

"What are you doing out at this time?"

They hovered in the hall, Kristina dumping her car keys into the bowl on the side table with a familiarity Parker couldn't help but like.

"Just finished work. Did I wake you?"

Parker shook her head.

"That makes pretty much…a twelve-hour shift. You must be tired. Did you eat? I can make you a—"

Cold lips covering her own killed the rest of the sentence.

"I'm not hungry for food, sweetheart."

Oh.

Kristina's fingers were cool when they wrapped around her throat, and Parker's breath caught. She was surprised she liked the gentle hold.

"I want to take you upstairs and fuck you. Would you like that?"

Fingers tweaked one of her nipples, and she jumped at the rough touch.

"Yes, Mistress."

The hand around her throat tightened ever so slightly before it let her go, and Kristina indicated for her to lead the way. Part of her objected, feeling selfish, greedy. Kristina had to be exhausted, and the urge to run her a bath and make her a midnight snack was strong.

A hand swatted Parker's behind on the way up the stairs, and she laughed, guilty that the desire to feel her, to be fucked by her, was stronger. *I'm an addict.*

Perched on the edge of her bed, she watched Kristina begin to undress, eyes tracking her every movement as with nimble fingers she flicked the clasp on her watch—*is that a freaking Rolex?*—and set it on the nightstand.

"Did I mention I've missed you?"

You did. Now Kristina was here, in her room, Parker realized she had missed her terribly in the week she had been almost completely absent from her life. Dark eyes flicked up to her face, and Kristina swallowed, her expression unreadable.

"Lie back on the bed and get naked for me."

Parker scooted back obediently, tugging her thin tank top over her head, letting her breasts fall free. Her plaid pants followed, and she lay back, enjoying the sight of Kristina wiggling her dress over her slim hips and kicking it to the floor.

"Are you wet for me?"

Parker wasn't sure. What she did notice was how comfortable she felt now, bare as she was before Kristina, at home in her body like she hadn't been at the start. *When did that happen?*

Kristina ran her hands up over her breasts, squeezing them, pushing them together in a display Parker was sure was for her benefit. Her body burned appreciatively.

"Touch yourself, baby, and tell me."

With her eyes on Kristina's, she slid her hand down her torso and between her legs, glad she'd decided to shave everything earlier that day.

She was. *Wow.* Kristina had barely been there five minutes, yet the effect on her was obvious.

"Well?"

The question was impatient, and a little piece of Parker enjoyed that. She circled herself a few times, daring to spread her legs a bit, watching Kristina's eyes flame at the view. She answered lazily.

"Yes, Mistress."

Kristina stalked toward the bed. Her knees hit the bottom of the mattress before she was crawling up and over her.

"Have you been taking care of your needs while I've been busy?"

Parker looked up at her. Tired as she was, she was still beautiful, sultry, sexy, in the blue glow of the muted TV. Dark hair cascaded over her shoulders. She still ached to kiss those full lips even without their usual red lipstick.

She confirmed she had, still rubbing herself slowly, her body growing hot from Kristina's proximity and the work of her own fingers.

"Good girl. Have you fucked yourself?"

She shook her head. Before, going inside while masturbating wasn't something she ever felt like, and now, it was something she resisted on purpose.

"Why not?"

Can I admit it?

She rubbed herself a little harder, feeling brave.

"I just..."

Kristina lowered herself down, and Parker felt a trail of hot slickness across her thigh as she ground against her. Parker reached up, enjoying the weight of full breasts in her hands.

"I like to keep that for you...only you."

She was momentarily embarrassed, but Kristina's reaction killed the feeling. The catch of her breath was audible, and the kiss that followed was hard, claiming, insistent.

"I like that, sweetheart."

Kristina's rough fingers batted hers away from herself and took over rubbing her.

"I like that, so much."

Teeth bit down hard on the muscle of Parker's shoulder; then a hot tongue soothed the ache. She groaned.

"Touch me, baby..."

Glad to oblige, Parker slipped a hand between them, pleased when her fingers slid easily between Kristina's legs.

"I missed this..."

The confession fell right into her mouth, and they were moving together, rubbing and grinding, and Parker felt the muscles in Kristina's back ripple as she dragged her fingers down it, tugging her impossibly closer.

"Do you want me in you?"

A tongue pushed rough into her mouth before she could answer, and she sucked it hard, nipping it with her teeth and enjoying the hiss as Kristina pulled it away.

Her legs were spread, her own arousal coating her thighs, Kristina's hand, the sheets, but she didn't care. This was desperate, dirty, and Kristina was right there with her, reveling in it all.

"Yes, Mistress. Please..."

A finger pushed into her, rough, and her back arched off the bed, everything in her pulling taut at the intrusion.

"Like that?"

She couldn't get the breath into her lungs to answer. Teeth grazed her nipple and she yelped.

"More."

Kristina laughed, the sound dark and heady. Parker forced her own hand to work faster, rubbing harder as a new wave of wetness coated her fingers.

"Ask me." Kristina was breathless.

"Please put two fingers inside me... Mistress..."

The last word became a moan as Kristina complied, working another inside her.

Parker's thighs were clenched tight, trapped open under the weight of Kristina's body above her. Fingers twisted in her hair, and her stomach jumped.

"I want to be inside you...please?"

Parker hadn't even planned to ask, didn't even acknowledge the thought until it was out there, between them. Kristina faltered, and then she was kissing her hard.

"Fine."

The fingers inside her curled, and Parker grit her teeth. She ignored the delicious high building low in her stomach, in favor of pulling back, looking up to watch Kristina's face while she slid a finger into her for the very first time.

Parker pushed the heel of her hand up against her and curled the digit, letting Kristina ride it.

When the movement between her own legs resumed, the pace was punishing, and Parker knew she wasn't going to last long like this.

They moved together, breaths mixing, sweat-soaked skin on skin. Kristina's arousal spilled over her hand, over her thigh, and she felt her own, slick around Kristina's fingers as they pumped her.

She was close, too close.

Reaching around, she grabbed Kristina's ass, kneading the soft flesh to urge her faster, harder against her hand. The walls around her finger fluttered in response, making her own body quiver.

"Come on, honey... Come for me."

Something flashed in Kristina's dark eyes at the words. It was the last thing Parker saw before her head fell back and she exploded, feeling Kristina jerking above her, still impaled on her finger as she did the same.

When Kristina collapsed on top of her, Parker held her tight as they rocked gently together, riding out the last of their mutual pleasure, before Kristina rolled half off her.

Tan fingers traced patterns over her shoulder, and Parker found herself combing through her dark hair, trying not to read into how much she enjoyed just being, existing, like this with her. Kristina's hair tickled her cheek as Parker lay on her back, Kristina curled into her side, her breathing steady, peaceful.

"Tired?"

Kristina only hummed in response.

"Can I ask you something?"

She hummed again and it sounded like agreement.

"How did you get into all this? I know you said you went through the agency…"

Kristina stiffened and was quiet for the longest time. Just when Parker wondered if she had fallen asleep, she replied, her voice soft, tired.

"You're right. I went through the agency, and that's how I met Mal. I went through her program, and she showed me a kind of intimacy I found acceptable after…" She looked away. "My time with her was important, because in learning how to submit, I came to understand what it takes to be a good Dominant."

Parker could sense her discomfort, the amount of effort it had taken for her to share even that much.

"That makes sense." She let her fingers card gently through her hair. "Are you staying?"

Kristina stiffened again at the question.

Parker leaned down to kiss her lips. She pulled away when she sensed Kristina was about to and tugged the comforter up around them.

"Honey, you're exhausted and it's so late for you to be driving home. Just stay."

She did.

"ARE YOU SURE I can't take you out for breakfast first?"

Kristina paused, dress up around her hips, bare from the waist up. Watching her lick her lips, Parker sensed her discomfort from her place in the bed.

"You know this is just sex, right, sweetheart?"

The words were careful, but it was easy to grasp the meaning behind them.

"I do." Parker kept her tone even. "But we've gone out to eat together before, and you're clearly exhausted and you've lost weight. Is it selfish that I want you healthy, Mistress?"

Kristina crossed the room and crawled back onto the bed and kissed her. It was chaste, and she felt Kristina smiling against her lips; then the kiss turned deeper, slow, and Parker couldn't help but wonder if Kristina knew this was just sex too.

Reluctantly, Parker kissed her once more and pulled away.

"Finish getting dressed and I'll make you a sandwich for the road?"

Kristina leaned in and kissed her once more.

"You're so good to me, Miss Freeman. That sounds nice, as long as you see me out the door."

Parker nodded her agreement, reluctantly leaving the warmth of the comforter to hunt for her pajamas.

"Parker..." Kristina's voice was low and delicious when she interrupted her search. "Don't put anything on."

Chapter Twelve

"DON'T FREAK OUT."

Parker leaned forward again, peering up at Kristina's house, wondering what was taking her so long.

"You're freaking me out with all this 'don't freak out'... What's going on?"

Marion sighed down the phone.

"So I was at work today..."

Parker hummed, drumming her fingers on the wheel, her eyes on the front door.

"Where exactly are you?" Marion asked.

Oops.

"Sorry, I'm at Kristina's, waiting to pick her up."

"Oh, going on a date?"

Parker tried to keep her feelings out of her voice. "No, she's having some work done at her place tomorrow, or something, so she's staying the night."

Tired of it idling, she turned off the engine.

"Okay, good. So I'm just going to come out and say it. The whole library benefit thing next week on campus, I think Amanda is going to be there."

"What?" She hissed the word. "Why would she even..."

"The hospital is making a show of donating, and they've been selling tickets this week. I talked to Ashley in phleb, and she told me Carol said Amanda bought two."

"Are you kidding me?"

Head back against the seat, Parker groaned. A flash of movement caught her eye, and she looked up to see Kristina's front door open, surprised when a woman stepped out onto the doorstep with her.

Kristina had a small duffel in her hands, and she looked as uncomfortable as Parker had ever seen her.

"Hello? You still there?"

"Yeah, sorry… Listen, I'll have to call you back, okay?"

Parker watched the pair as they walked down the path. Kristina looked stiff, wary, her face painted in grim lines.

"Okay, fine, but just ask her."

"Wait, ask who what?"

A few strides away from the car, the woman pulled Kristina in for a hug. Parker tried to ignore the flare of annoyance in her chest. She was gorgeous, maybe a few years Kristina's senior, with carefully straightened hair and heavily made-up eyes. She looked like a model, and Parker felt plain, and old, in comparison.

"Kristina, ask her to go to the benefit with you, to stick it to Amanda."

Her stomach lurched, and she wasn't sure if it was from the mention of her ex-wife, or the woman who was now sliding down into her ostentatious red convertible. Parker grimaced as gravel sprayed her windshield as the car pulled out of the driveway.

"Okay, M, gotta go, love you. Kiss Roland for me."

She ended the call as Kristina tugged open the passenger door. The smile on her face didn't reach her eyes.

"Hey, sweetheart."

For the first time, the endearment sounded hollow. Parker told herself to relax, though alarm bells were screaming in her mind.

"Hi. How are you?"

She didn't wait for Kristina to kiss her as she sometimes did lately, or even expect a real answer. She pulled out down the driveway, the large metal gates closing behind them as she headed back to the street.

Kristina was looking out of the window, too quiet.

"I'm glad things are still settling down at work. Did you get whatever the holdup was on Wednesday figured out?"

The question worked like she'd hoped it might, and Kristina dived into talking about delayed shipments and incompetent staff, and the air in the car was suddenly less thick.

Parker nodded in the right places, taking her eyes off the road to watch her, leaning back in the seat now, running her fingers through her dark hair, pulling it back from her face.

"So who was that?"

She felt the shift in atmosphere like it was physical.

"Is that really any of your business?"

Though she'd known Kristina would be defensive, sensed that something was up with her visitor, she hadn't expected such a harsh reaction.

Returning her eyes to the road, she gunned the engine when the light changed. First Amanda, now this. She had hoped for a better start to the weekend.

"No, I guess it's not."

The drive back to her place was stony, silent, and when she unbuckled her seat belt, Kristina didn't move.

"Would you prefer if I went home?"

The question didn't seem sullen, just tired.

Would I? Parker knew she was pissed about the Amanda situation, that her ex was obviously inserting herself into her life again—was she letting that color how she felt about Kristina?

"No...I'm sorry." She could be the bigger person. "I just had a bad day. I apologize."

For a second, she thought, hoped, Kristina was going to apologize too, but a long beat passed between them, and then, with a nod, she opened the passenger door.

They were barely inside before Kristina paused on the stairs.

"Mind if I take a shower?"

The request confused Parker, but she recovered quickly.

"Sure, you know where it is. Help yourself to whatever you need, okay?"

Kristina was already climbing the stairs again.

"Kristina..." Those dark eyes found her from the top. "Is the water off at your place because of the work or...?"

Parker watched her swallow, then nod, then disappear down the hall.

Kristina was acting weird. *Who the hell was that woman?*

The two cups of coffee she'd taken her time with making were stone cold on the counter, and Parker could still hear the water running upstairs. Giving up on standing there in the kitchen, organizing her spice rack for the fourth time and turning it all over in her head— Amanda, Kristina, the unknown woman—she headed upstairs.

The only sound from her bathroom was the spray hitting the tub, the door cracked. She hovered by it, and then decided.

Things had been better lately. Kristina's company was over the worst of whatever crisis had kept her so busy, and they'd just been getting back to their easy rhythm.

This weekend was something Parker had looked forward to, and she was eager to pull it back from the rapid decline it had taken. With her clothes on the floor, she pushed open the bathroom door.

A month ago there was no way she would have been brave enough to do this. Though her heart beat hard, she was proud she dared.

"Kristina?"

She tapped on the glass pane of the shower, before she slid it back and poked her head around. Kristina turned sideways, almost hiding herself, and the action shook Parker to her core.

"Mind if I come in?"

Parker saw her piecing herself together, twisting a smile onto her lips, letting her hands fall slack by her sides, shoulders back to proudly display her body as she usually did.

"Not at all."

Kristina looked young, her dark hair turned ebony, slicked back by the water, her face clean of makeup. Something in Parker's chest tugged at the sight, because she was still disarmingly beautiful.

As she inched closer, the fine hair on her arms raised in the cool of the stall. Kristina watched, and the moment was still heavy, something still hanging between them, naked as they were in front of each other.

"Can I kiss you?"

Kristina's bottom lip was between her teeth, and Parker felt her consider it, before finally, she nodded. Everything in her wanted to step up to her, sweet and slow, tug her body against her and kiss her soft, careful. Licking her lips, she forced herself not to linger, not to push Kristina any further when she was clearly already shaken.

As if they belonged to a stranger, she watched her own pale fingers run up Kristina's tan chest, over her collarbone, and up around the back of her neck to tug her in. The hot spray rained down over them, and Kristina was quiet under her mouth, pliable in a way she rarely was.

Parker didn't know who closed the distance, but they pressed together, her own skin growing wet, her hair soaking flat down her back under the water. Kristina's hands settled around her wrists, their lips slid together, tongues brushing close, and Parker had no idea if those hands were there to keep her close or ready to push her away.

She waited for Kristina to balk, to push her back or spin them around and shove her against the wall. She waited for the fingers on her wrists to get rough, to twist in her hair, move firm against her body, but they never did. Everything between them was spilling, deep and slow and slipping into a territory that was only vaguely familiar, and last time they'd been here, Kristina had run.

Stepping back, Parker searched her dark eyes. Kristina just looked back at her, rivulets of water rolling down her slim neck, over her shoulders.

"Can I ask who that was at your house?"

Parker saw her steel herself.

"That was Mal."

It took her a second to recognize the name of the woman who'd been Kristina's Dominant.

"She was your—"

Kristina nodded before she could finish.

"I guess you don't want to talk about it?"

She shook her head, and Parker conceded with a kiss, ready to comfort her in the only way she knew how, through a language she'd known before they'd met, but over the last few months, Kristina had made her fluent in. She wondered if Kristina knew sex could be more than a game, more than a weapon.

"Parker."

She was surprised when gentle hands on her biceps tugged her away.

"What was wrong with you? Earlier, you seemed tense."

Right. We're sharing. She swallowed. The last thing she wanted to think about right now was Amanda, but it only seemed fair.

"Remember the library benefit your buddy the dean came to talk to me about? Well, Marion told me Amanda's going to be there, probably with her girlfriend, so..."

Would Kristina think it was shallow, pathetic that she cared?

"If it upsets you, maybe you shouldn't go?"

It was a good solution and she wished it was so easy.

"I have to. The library will largely benefit my department and the dean is expecting all the professors to attend."

Eager for something else to do, Parker reached around her for the shampoo.

"What are you afraid of?"

Kristina caught the bottle before she could turn it up and dump some of the liquid into her hand.

Her mouth felt suddenly dry.

"I'm..." She had to search herself for a second before she could grasp the honest answer. "I'm afraid of how it's going to look, her with her new, young, girlfriend who she cheated on me openly with for years, and me alone, again. I'm afraid it's going to be humiliating, and the worst part is this is an event for *my* workplace, that's important for *my* career. I can't think why she'd decide to come if not to rub things in my face."

Kristina was watching her. She tried to take the shampoo back, but Kristina held it firm.

"I could go with you."

Marion is freaking psychic.

"You want to go with me to the benefit, as my girlfriend, to save me from total humiliation in front of my bitch ex-wife?"

Kristina took a deep breath and nodded, tipping her head back and letting the shower soak her hair again.

"To pretend to be your girlfriend, yes. I can do that for you, sweetheart. If you want."

Parker should be grateful, happy even that she had a solution. Kristina was young, she was gorgeous, and the dean already thought they were together anyway, yet disappointment settled heavy in her stomach instead.

She forced herself to smile.

"Okay."

KRISTINA'S WEALTH STILL caught her off guard. Somewhere over the last few months she had become just Kristina, with her yoga pants and the ability to see Parker completely undone with barely more than a sentence.

When Parker stepped out of the fancy dark car, with an honest-to-God driver holding the door open for them, she was definitely reminded that Kristina was well off.

"Ready?"

Kristina was eye level with her in ridiculously high heels, stunning in a floor-length black dress. If not for the way those dark eyes watched her appreciatively, the look on her face when she'd opened the door earlier that night, Parker might feel plain beside her.

"As I'll ever be."

She tried to ignore the way her heart stuttered as Kristina took her hand and led her through the double doors into the hall where the benefit was being held.

The sheer size of the event struck her. There had to be three hundred people in the large space, at least. Tables and chairs took up one half of the room, two bars in the other and a stage up front. Combing through bodies, Parker searched for anyone she knew.

"Wow. They are disgustingly cute."

She followed Kristina's line of sight and couldn't help but laugh at Marion, beautiful in a red dress, LiLing twirling her slowly to the barely audible music, dapper in a fitted pantsuit, her hair piled high on her head in an elegant twist.

"Yep, they're pretty much like that all the time."

If Kristina heard the envy in her voice, she didn't comment.

"Kristina Diaz."

An older man Parker didn't recognize approached them and introduced his wife.

"Maurice, it's so nice to see you. This is my partner, Professor Parker Freeman."

Parker didn't know how many times her heart could take hearing Kristina introduce her like that tonight.

The woman in question tugged her close and pressed a kiss to her cheek that made her blush.

"Sweetheart, why don't you go say hi to Marion? I'll be over in just a minute."

Kristina gave her an out and, thankful, Parker took it.

With one last long look at the stunning creature who was her *pretend* date for the night, she left to weave through bodies. A couple of faces registered as familiar, and she said a few quick hellos, before finally, she made it to her friends.

"Wow... Look at you!" LiLing greeted her with a hug.

"Where is she?" Marion pulled her in next. "If she stood you up..."

"Easy, mama bear, she's here. She didn't stand me up. She did pick me up in some fancy car with a driver and champagne." Parker couldn't help but feel a little giddy as she relayed that particular development.

Marion squealed predictably. "So I finally get to meet her on a night when I'm not having to take drastic action for you two idiots and suck face with you?"

Parker nodded.

"I don't even want to know."

Parker reached up and adjusted LiLing's collar, eyes apologetic. "Your wife very graciously assaulted my mouth, all for the greater good of course."

LiLing laughed—the woman was a freaking saint. Parker glanced to Marion, a smile on her lips, surprised her best friend's face had turned hard.

"Look at you..."

Parker spun around. She would know that voice anywhere.

"Amanda..." She paused, letting her eyes fall to the woman at her side. "Emily."

She tried to collect herself, her heartbeat erratic, the color draining out of her cheeks as her ex-wife's eyes swept over her. She found her voice, all her courage, anger from their last meeting long gone now. "What a surprise to see you here."

She could be cordial.

"Yes, and not much of a surprise to see *you* here, I suppose. Still the eternal plus one for Mrs. and Mrs. Hua?" Amanda asked.

Parker swallowed hard, hate burning in her throat. Before she could grit out a reply, Amanda continued speaking.

"You look good, Parker. Are you running again?"

She sensed Marion take a breath and knew the woman was about to explode.

"There you are, sweetheart..." Kristina was suddenly in her space, stepping up to her and kissing her full on the mouth, her lips lingering for a few seconds longer than was strictly appropriate.

"Oh, excuse me." Kristina stepped back, the picture of etiquette as she pretended to notice Amanda. Parker couldn't help but watch Emily's eyes on Kristina.

"Amanda, this is Kristina Diaz."

She couldn't bring herself to say the words. She didn't have to.

"Amanda, it's nice to finally meet you. I'm Parker's partner." Her tone was polite but icy, and it was clear Kristina was no stranger to politics. "And this must be Emily." The hint of condescension in her voice was absolute gold. Any other time Parker might have laughed, but she knew Amanda well enough to recognize her hackles rising.

"Kristina..." Amanda's voice was low, mocking. "Isn't it a little past your bedtime?"

Parker opened her mouth, but Kristina was faster, one hand on her waist, tugging her close as she turned to her.

"What do you think, sweetheart? We did have an awfully late night last night. Well, I guess it was more like this morning by the time there was any actual sleeping. But I think I can hold out a bit longer; how about you?"

Her dark eyes were shining, that hand on Parker's hip was holding her soft, possessive, and all of it was so surreal. She had to clear her throat before she could agree she was good. Kristina turned back to Amanda, totally unfazed.

"Nope, looks like we're okay right now. Have to say though, I love the décor in the master. Did you choose the color scheme, or was that Parker?"

Amanda looked like she was choking on air. Parker knew from years of experience she was so used to intimidating people, so used to people backing down to her brashness, her rudeness, that there was absolutely nothing behind it.

Emily tugged on her hand, but Amanda's blue eyes were busy burning into her.

"What, did you hire her to come here with you? If I look her up am I going to find her on some high-end escort website?"

Parker's cheeks flamed. Amanda was not being quiet, and somehow, the words felt just a little too close to the truth.

Emily tugged Amanda's hand again, and Amanda pulled it away. Parker almost felt sorry for her. She'd been there.

"Amanda, I think your girlfriend has something to say."

A muscle in the woman's throat jumped as she turned to Kristina, and God, Parker did not miss her temper. She'd been glad when by the end, Amanda didn't even care about her enough to be mad anymore.

"It's *Doctor Miller* to you, Krystal." Parker knew her use of the incorrect name was deliberate.

Kristina laughed, sounding to all the world like she found all this thrilling. Then suddenly, she was deadly serious.

"Doctor Miller, Emily has something to say, but if you won't give her the time of day, perhaps you'll give it to me. I believe what she's trying to tell you is that she wants to leave now because unlike you, she knows I am in fact the multimillionaire who owns the company where her father is currently a midranking executive, and I'm guessing Frank has no idea you're in a relationship with his daughter."

This is happening. Parker had never seen someone dismantle Amanda so thoroughly, not in all their years together, and the color on Amanda's cheeks as she looked between Emily and Kristina was priceless.

"So high-paid escort, no. I'm just here for a good night, to support my beautiful girlfriend's workplace, and probably make a hefty donation toward the new library. So unless there's anything else, I'd like to get back to that?"

Amanda's face was scarlet as she was dismissed. When she stormed away, one last scoff in Parker's direction, Emily stayed, looking like she might burst into tears.

"Miss Diaz... Please don't tell him."

Kristina looked at her, face impassive. "I don't care who you fuck—frankly, it's none of my business—but when you break into my partner's house, it becomes personal."

Tears spilled onto Emily's cheeks, and Parker felt bad, despite herself. She should be jumping for joy right now, but she couldn't help but wonder why Emily was so upset. Was her dad a homophobe?

"Treat us with respect, and we'll extend you the same courtesy. That includes not telling your father, understood?"

Emily nodded, offering her a watery thank-you, before she scurried off after Amanda.

Kristina raised her glass to her lips, and Parker just looked at her, stunned. Marion seemed to recover first.

"Okay, I like her; we're definitely keeping her."

Parker's cheeks flamed.

OF COURSE, KRISTINA was the perfect girlfriend. She connected instantly with Marion and seemed to win LiLing's respect, and the meshing of the two worlds was so surreal to Parker.

A hand settled on the small of her back, and soft lips brushed her ear as Kristina leaned in to ask if she was having fun.

She nodded, clutching the bar, trying to ignore the horrible twisting in her stomach.

All of it had been perfect. Kristina was smart, she was funny, she won over even the most conservative professors who Parker knew had avoided her in the past for her sexuality, despite being sixteen years younger, *and* a woman.

"You seem tense, baby..."

Soft lips brushed the hollow of her throat, and she squeezed her eyes closed. Kristina was so attentive, so perfectly supportive, almost loving, and Parker hated it because she wished it was real.

Swallowing it down, she turned to look at her, trying to see her as temporary, as sex, as an arrangement. The dark eyes she had come to know were looking back at her, heavy with concern, soft and warm and open. She looked away.

"Tell me, Parker."

That voice sent prickles across the back of her neck, and sex was familiar, it was *allowed*, and she threw herself down that route with all she had, because the other, it could only end in disaster.

"I just want you."

All of you, not just the sex.

Kristina took the words exactly as she knew she would, gaze falling to Parker's lips as she licked her own.

"Want to leave?"

She nodded.

Kristina's hands stayed on her, at her waist, her hip, the small of her back, as they moved through the thinning crowds, eventually saying good night to the dean, who thanked Kristina again for the check Parker had purposefully looked away while she wrote, and then Marion and LiLing.

Kristina had graciously offered them a ride, but their cab was already waiting. Parker heard her talking quietly to LiLing, while Marion pulled her in for a hug.

"I like her."

Parker squeezed her best friend tight, trying to draw some strength, some clarity, from her.

"Me too…"

Marion's arms tightened around her. When they pulled apart she looked up at her, and Parker knew she knew.

"She makes an awfully good girlfriend for someone who doesn't date."

Wrapping her arms around herself, cold in the late night air, Parker nodded her agreement. She waited, watching until the two were in their cab, pulling out of sight.

"Come on, sweetheart, you're cold..."

Kristina took her hand and led her to where their own car was waiting. She opened the door for her and let her slide in first.

How am I ever supposed to not want this?

SHEETS WERE SOFT underneath her; the metal of the cuffs around her wrists was cold.

She opened her eyes and the room spun pleasantly, the three glasses of champagne she'd drunk on the way back here doing their job.

"Is this what you wanted?"

Kristina was hovering above her, her hair tickling Parker's neck and shoulder where it fell over her, those dark eyes smoldering down at her.

"Yes."

She purposefully omitted the title, knowing Kristina would retaliate, and push this harder, darker, into a space where there was no room for thinking anymore. Kristina leaned down, and Parker's lips parted automatically, expecting a kiss. Teeth closed around her lower lip, tugging it hard.

When it was released she ran her tongue over the indented flesh, thankful she didn't taste any blood.

Kristina's eyes were searching hers.

"Yes, Mistress."

Parker smirked with the words and dark fire lit in Kristina's eyes. It was almost as if she knew Parker wanted this rough, quick, clean. Kristina pulled back from the kiss at the last second and dipped her head again, leaving Parker with her head back, eyes closed, wanting.

Lips attached themselves instead to her throat, kissing, nipping, sucking their way down. Cool fingers trailed the inside of her arms, and then nails raked back along their path, following the contour of her muscles, pulled taut, arms stretched as she was held by the handcuffs to the headboard.

Kristina rained down delicious torture on her, with her mouth, hands, nails, and teeth. Parker felt like every inch of her skin had been touched, teased, tasted. Her nipples strained uncomfortably. She was wet, hot, sticky, sweat trickling down into her hair, pinned under the weight of Kristina's body, as she continued to torture her. Teeth nipped high on the inside of her thigh, and her body jumped off the bed.

"Need something?"

Kristina's eyes snapped up, and Parker took a deep breath through her nose. Usually she'd try being sweet, polite, asking her to touch her, but the liquor still buzzed in her veins and the confusion of the evening, all her feelings, were still too close. For once, Kristina wasn't taking her out of her head fast enough.

She took a deep breath.

"Yes, Mistress."

A tongue traced the seam of her thigh, and she had to squeeze her eyes closed, her hips canting up, body clenching frustratingly on nothing.

"What is it, sweetheart?"

The endearment twisted her. Dark as it was, even like this, she said it with so much care. Like Parker was special, more than just one more in a line of many, one more arrangement that would come to an end the minute she admitted somehow, she'd developed feelings.

She locked the thought down.

"Are you going to fuck me or just tease me all night?"

She hadn't meant to snap. Kristina's gaze turned watchful, and she hated it. She just wanted to forget.

"Okay, red, time out. Is something wrong?"

Kristina was crawling up the bed, and Parker wanted to groan, to sigh, to freaking scream. Never did she imagine Kristina would be the first of them to use the safe word.

Soft fingers touched her cheek, and Parker had to take a deep breath to keep the touch from breaking her open.

"Want me to let you out?"

She shook her head.

"No, Kristina, I just..." She reached to run a hand through her hair. The cuff bit the soft flesh on the inside of her wrist, reminding her she couldn't. "I want you to fuck me. That's what this is, right, that's what we do? We just fuck?"

Kristina didn't reply. She reached over and set one of Parker's wrists free, and soon the other followed. Parker was horribly, irrationally angry at the development.

"You're not in the right headspace for this."

Fury burned hot in her chest.

"Do not tell me how I feel."

Kristina tossed the handcuffs on the bed, and Parker sensed her discomfort; then in a second it was gone and her expression was guarded.

"Did I do something wrong tonight?"

Parker bit her lip, sitting up. Part of her was aware they were having this conversation naked, but she didn't care.

"No, you didn't do anything wrong. It was perfect... You were perfect." She laughed a bitter little sound and heard Kristina take a breath. Looking up, she watched her face fall.

"You want more."

Parker hated the sad note of acceptance in her voice.

"And you don't?" She hadn't meant to make it a question. She hadn't meant to tell her any of this, but here they were.

"I don't date, sweetheart. I don't get involved beyond—"

"Oh bullshit, Kristina. Maybe you just didn't notice, but we date."

Kristina looked horrified, like the words were an accusation.

"We have a relationship outside of sex. You were the picture-perfect girlfriend tonight; you just... Don't tell me you can't."

Parker swallowed hard. Everything was falling off track, so suddenly horribly, derailed, and she didn't know how to go back or make it stop. She didn't know if she wanted to.

"Parker, I was honest with you from the start. And I never told you I can't, but I won't. I don't want to..."

Rejection burned hot in her chest. They were good together, terribly, wonderfully good. How did Kristina not see that; how did she not want it too?

"So this is all just a part of it then? All the pet names and the sleepovers, the text messages, the cuddling?"

Kristina looked appalled.

"I don't..."

She shot up off the bed with a curse. Parker watched her pace, tucking her hands under her knees because they were shaking with the adrenaline.

"I've never been with anyone like this... There. I said it. I do break all my own rules with you, Parker, and it's fucking terrifying."

She crossed her arms over her chest and turned to walk back to the bed.

"If we already do all that, then what's the problem? According to you we already have more, so what are you asking me for?"

All of it. Selfishly, Parker wanted all of her. More than just an arrangement, more than just the promise of right now.

Kristina was watching her, hovering halfway between the bed and the door, and she looked so vulnerable.

Parker pushed to her feet and crossed the room to her. She reached for her and tugged her in. Holding her close, she took a deep breath, trying to let go of the darkness, the bitterness, trying to find some hope that somehow, this could work. Her fingertips skimmed Kristina's cheek, brushing back dark hair before she leaned down slowly and pressed their lips together.

The pads of Kristina's fingers grazed the tops of her arms as she kissed her, holding her close, and then they pushed her away.

"Parker..."

Kristina looked sad and sorry, and smaller than Parker had ever seen.

"I don't want to lose our arrangement."

Parker swallowed hard.

"I don't want to lose you either."

Why does this feel so much like goodbye?

"Then don't. Can't we just enjoy this for what it is? Because that's the only option, sweetheart."

Parker hated the tears pricking at the back of her eyes.

"So dating you, counting on you being a part of my life going forward with any sort of certainty, is off the table? We just keep doing this on the understanding that we will until we're not sexually compatible anymore, or one of us decides to end it? And then you'll just be gone?"

Kristina looked grave as she nodded, and embarrassingly, one of Parker's tears spilled over.

"Baby..." Kristina stepped into her, and it was so unfair; she was so confusing. "I don't plan on going anywhere anytime soon. As long as you can respect my limits and I know you understand our arrangement, I'm gonna be here, okay?"

Kristina wrapped her slim arms around her, and Parker wanted to shove her away as much as she wanted to let herself melt into her. Fingers pushed into her hair, scratching her scalp, and she let her chin rest on Kristina's shoulder. They fit together, and somehow she felt right, safe, like she belonged there.

Given the choice between keeping what they had, or losing her completely, there wasn't really a choice at all.

Kristina held her until they were both breathing easier, steady. When she stepped back there was a smile on her face, though something sad still echoed in her dark eyes.

Careful fingers reached up to wipe the tears from her cheeks.

"Wanna go to IHOP?"

Parker couldn't help but laugh.

Chapter Thirteen

"SO SHE FLAT out said no?"

The café was busy around them, the lunchtime rush just leaving. Parker looked out of the window, eyes flitting from passerby to passerby, wondering about their stories, if they were anything like as complex as her own, with her kinky almost girlfriend.

"Basically. She doesn't do relationships, but she doesn't want to lose what we have."

Marion hummed across the table, and the sound disappointed her, because somehow, she still wanted her to like Kristina.

"I don't even know what to say. I mean at the benefit she was just, wow, and she's gorgeous, funny, rich... But the commitment issues are..."

"Terminal?" Parker offered the word, deadpan.

Marion winced.

"It just makes no sense. She was so..."

She clapped her hands together, one squeezing the other tight, clinging.

Parker nodded.

"I know."

She did.

"It's like when she forgets herself and that she's supposed to be this no-relationships deal, it's just..."

"Good?" Marion asked.

"Yeah, really good."

Marion reached a tan hand across the table to squeeze her own.

"I'm so sorry, sweetie. What are you going to do? I know you always envisioned settling down and..."

Parker was glad she didn't say kids. She didn't want to open that can of worms, not today. She gently took her hand back and picked up her fork.

"I don't know."

She didn't.

"All my life I did want to just...settle...and then I met Amanda and clung so hard to settling that I threw fifteen years down the drain. And now, all I want is her."

She swallowed hard, pushing the remainder of her salad around the plate.

"But there's no future?"

The question was tentative, careful, but it had needed to be asked. She shrugged.

"I don't know. She says she does want to continue as we are, and I mean, we're almost in a relationship, but what happens when one day she gets bored of the sex, or decides we're not compatible anymore...whatever that means?"

She felt Marion weighing in, trying to wrap her mind around the situation so she could give the best advice.

"Maybe you should try dating? Just see what else is out there, see if she really is worth sticking with for now... I mean she was always meant to be temporary."

The words hurt, and Parker raised her eyes, hating that there were tears in them.

"But she's... I don't know, she's...Kristina."

Marion's face fell, the corners of her mouth creasing with concern.

"Oh, sweetie."

Panic flared in Parker's chest.

"Are you... Do you...love her?"

It was the question she'd been avoiding asking herself, the one she was afraid to answer, because she just couldn't.

"No, of course not. I just... I found myself through her and she's gorgeous like you said, and we just work, but no... I just like what we have."

Marion nodded, but her mouth was set in a grim line Parker chose to ignore, before she recovered.

"Well, Lucy in cardiology always had a crush on you. She's been single for a while now."

Parker's automatic reaction was no, and it must have showed on her face.

"I just mean if you want to try things out, see if you're ready to move on and let Kristina go for something with the potential to be permanent. She's a good option."

Her heart twisted painfully. She didn't want to let Kristina go, but logically, it was the right choice, the rational choice. After so many bad decisions, maybe for once, she should try being rational.

"I'll think about it."

She knew to Marion, her answer was as good as a yes.

Walking back to campus, she tried so hard not to think about Kristina, about the things she saw in her dark eyes when Kristina thought she wasn't looking, the softness of the hands in her hair when she thought she was asleep.

Her phone buzzed, and she tugged it out of her pocket, half expecting it to be Marion telling her she'd set her up on a date already.

Her stomach flipped guiltily.

Just landed. New York is beautiful, it would be more beautiful with you.

Just like that, the thought that Lucy could ever hold a candle to her was long gone. Kristina was on a business trip. Parker hadn't expected to hear from her until next week, but just that simple, one-line message lifted her up and broke her apart.

It was so obvious even she couldn't ignore it.

She was falling for Kristina.

They lingered on her doorstep, awkward. Parker pushed her keys into the lock and turned back to say good night. Lucy stepped forward, and Parker stepped into her. She'd gone this far, and now she was comfortable to let herself explore this. Emotionally, she wasn't Kristina. The kiss was flat, messy, and made it clear that physically, sexually, she wasn't either.

Lucy pulled away with a laugh.

"I'm sorry. I've thought you were just gorgeous forever and could never understand why you were with a prick like Miller, but that was..."

Parker laughed out loud.

"Not the best for you either?"

Lucy shook her head.

"You're not in love with her, are you?"

Heat jumped in Parker's chest, a flare of panic.

"Amanda, I mean, still?"

She exhaled with a laugh.

"No...God no... Hell no!"

She liked Lucy, with her kind blue eyes and crooked smile; she was charming and sweet, but she just wasn't *her*.

"But there is someone?"

God, I feel like a horrible person.

"Lucy... I'm sorry. It's complicated. I really did want to see where things led tonight."

"It's all right." She shoved her hands in her pockets with a shrug and a grin. "I guess I was always just meant to admire you from the nurses' station. Anything more simply isn't supposed to be." She took a step back off the porch. "I hope it works out though, whoever it's complicated with. She's a hell of a lucky woman."

Parker watched until Lucy was in the car and then stepped into the house. Something heavy sat in her chest, and it hurt. Retrieving her phone, she plopped down onto the stairs in the dark.

I'm in love with Kristina. God, I'm in love, again... The staccato rhythm of her heart, the giddy little butterflies, and the burn of anxiety in her gut, they were all familiar, and all things she thought she'd outgrown long ago.

Screw it.

She opened up Kristina's message, and she typed.

> *I went on a date tonight. She was funny and kind. We didn't have sex, so you can relax. It should have been good, but it wasn't.*

She hit Send and took a deep breath.

> *Because she wasn't you. Sweet dreams, honey. Fly safe tomorrow and come back to me.*

By the time she was in bed, plugging her phone in to charge overnight, ready to sleep, there was still no reply.

Chapter Fourteen

SHE KNOCKED ON Kristina's familiar front door. The sun was setting behind her, and she'd received the text from her at the airport asking to meet almost as soon as she landed.

Butterflies swirled in her stomach, and she knocked again. When nobody answered, she tried the door on instinct. The handle moved and it creaked open.

"Kristina?"

She stepped inside and closed the door behind her, the first hints of worry trickling into her stomach, turning the butterflies it touched to dust.

She called for Kristina again, relieved that as she walked down the hall, she heard her voice somewhere at the end. Tucking her hair back behind her ear, smoothing her hands over the tight jeans around her thighs, Parker stepped into the kitchen.

Kristina was pacing, one arm around her middle, the other holding her cell to her ear, a language spilling from her lips so quickly it took Parker a minute to recognize it as Spanish.

Kristina's dark eyes snapped to her, and she smiled, suddenly nervous. *Am I intruding?*

"Listen, I have to call you back."

The voice on the other end of the line was still talking—Parker heard them calling what sounded like "Kris"—when she ended the call and tossed the cell onto the counter.

"Parker."

She strode toward her, black jeans and high boots, a deep-red sweater that fell down just low enough to show her sculpted collarbone and a sliver of black bra strap.

"Mistress..."

Parker bit her lip as she delivered the greeting, enjoying the instant response it gained. With Kristina momentarily knocked off balance, she took the opening and ran with it.

"So, your friends call you Kris?"

Recovering, Kristina shook her head. "No, he's a dick. He calls me that because he knows I hate it."

"I see." Parker reached up to catch Kristina's chin, stepping into her space and using the height advantage for all it was worth. She didn't know how she'd suddenly acquired the upper hand, but she planned to enjoy it for as long as it lasted.

"So what *do* your friends call you, Miss Diaz?"

She leaned down to brush her lips against Kristina's full ones, though the action wasn't a kiss.

"Kristina, Boss, I know one beautiful woman who calls me Mistress... That's all."

Parker kissed her softly, nipping at her bottom lip before she pulled away.

"Once upon a time, when I was a kid, my friends called me Krissie."

She wasn't sure who was more surprised by the information being shared, her or Kristina, but she instantly liked the nickname.

Pulling back, she studied Kristina's face.

"Would you hate if I called you that, from time to time?"

Kristina swallowed hard, and her expression shifted, and Parker knew her time leading the game was coming to an end.

"No, I don't think I would, but I'd prefer you call me Mistress…"

This time it was Kristina who leaned in to initiate the kiss, her tongue that pushed into Parker's mouth, seeking, claiming. Just as she was melting, ready to peel herself out of her clothes and let Kristina have her right there on the kitchen floor, Kristina pulled back.

"You went on a date."

Parker's breath caught, her tongue darting out across her kiss-swollen lips.

"I did."

Why do I feel so guilty?

"How was it?"

Kristina's voice was dark and demanding, and Parker knew she already knew the answer. If she wanted to hear her say it, she would. Forcing her gaze up to Kristina's face, she took a deep breath.

"She wasn't you."

The tension in the room was thick, heavy. Kristina looked frozen, scared, and so uncertain that Parker reached up to smooth back her hair and then gave her an out.

"I'd rather go to IHOP."

They both laughed.

"I think you have a crush on that poor unsuspecting waitress, Miss Freeman."

Just like that, Kristina was back.

Parker kicked off her shoes and shed her jacket, slowly, confidently, letting it fall to the floor before she looked back to Kristina. Though her actions oozed sex, her admission was shy, softer.

"I think I have a crush on you."

A beat passed between them, and then they were inching forward, closing the distance, slow, tentative. Parker watched Kristina's eyes fall closed, felt the uncertainty in the gentle press of her lips, the tremble in her fingers when they slid soft up her waist.

That kiss was sweet and slow, and so heartbreakingly honest. Parker's body reacted as strong as it always did, but she didn't want to fuck her; she wanted to lay her down and worship her.

"Parker..." Kristina pulled back just barely, their foreheads resting against each other, their breaths the only sound in the quiet of the kitchen.

"I know, honey..."

Parker swallowed down the emotion thick in her throat.

"Take me to bed, Mistress?"

Kristina hovered, one hand still in Parker's hair, her lips parted, and she was sure she was going to say something; she could see it in her eyes, see the moment she lost her nerve and it died. She licked her lips instead.

"As you wish, sweetheart."

Somewhere along the way it had become a race. Parker skidded into the bedroom on her socked feet, Kristina one pace behind her, laughing.

"Is this the part where I get to claim my prize?"

Parker turned back to her, but Kristina was already advancing.

"I think this is the part where you repent for your sins."

Her stomach flipped. Kristina's tan fingers closed around her throat and pushed her back onto the bed, and then they were kissing, rough and messy. Parker reached up to feel the weight of Kristina's breasts in her hands, squeezing them firmly. Fingers in her hair tugged her head back. They were both panting.

"You went on a date."

Parker laughed. She couldn't help it.

"I thought you don't do jealousy."

Kristina swallowed hard.

"So did I."

Something passed between them, and hot as she was, wet, excited, and freaking intoxicated to be back with Kristina, to be laughing, Parker didn't want to let it kill their moment.

"So what, are you going to spank me again?"

She let the challenge echo in her eyes. Kristina's nostrils flared.

"No, that would be unoriginal now you asked, and while I was away I had plenty of time to think of what to do with my *bad girl*, when I got home."

God, I should not like that as much as I do.

"I'm going to fuck you, in a way I've always wanted to. Unless you're not comfortable and would prefer another spanking."

She was disappointed when Kristina climbed off her, disappeared into the closet, and reappeared with something in her hands.

"Sit up."

She pushed herself up, leaning close to Kristina when she sat down beside her.

"How do you feel about toys?"

She studied the purple thing in Kristina's hand, trying to figure out how it worked.

"Here. Hold it."

She put her hand out obediently and gripped the thing when it hit her palm. It was soft, a little squishy, one side was longer, and she could imagine where that went. The bulb on the other end was more troublesome.

"I, um, I'm not sure I'm comfortable with anything in my..." She poked the bulb awkwardly.

Kristina moved closer, catching her chin, amusement shining in her eyes as she forced Parker to meet them.

"Say it."

Parker licked her lips, her cheeks flaming. Tears pricked her eyes unexpectedly, as she realized with a jolt this could be the thing that made them incompatible.

"Hey."

Kristina took the toy from her hands and tossed it on the bed, then pulled her into a hug, all the amusement gone.

"What is it?"

Gentle hands stroked her hair, and Parker let herself be held.

"I've never done...anything like...anal. I could try. I just..." She swallowed.

"Parker." Kristina tugged her back, holding her around the top of her arms. "It's a strapless dildo. The short side goes in me; the other side is what I'd like to fuck you with, in the same place I always fuck you."

Parker felt her pulse in her face, mortified, and Kristina was laughing. She shoved her away.

"No...sweetheart, no. You're just adorable."

"I hate you."

She tried to look everywhere, anywhere but at Kristina.

"I was so worried if I said I didn't know you'd think we weren't compatible."

She heard her take a breath.

"Parker, I don't ever want you to worry about telling me something makes you uncomfortable. That will never change our compatibility."

She tried to be relieved at Kristina's assurance, but she was still just embarrassed.

"Look at me..."

She couldn't.

"Look at me, right now." Taking a deep breath, she turned, surprised when Kristina kissed her.

"We're compatible. More compatible than I've ever experienced with anyone." Kristina settled a hand over her breast, rubbing, squeezing pleasantly. "You're beautiful, and sexy, and you make me work for it. You don't care about the money, and things with you are just wonderfully, disarmingly easy. It's not something you have to worry about, okay?"

Licking her lips, a few tears drying on her cheeks, Parker nodded.

"You hiding how you feel or not being honest with me will hurt things faster than you ever being uncomfortable with something and saying so will. Understand?"

She nodded again, falling easily when Kristina pushed her back. Lips kissed her cheek, then settled against her ear.

"If you ever feel ready, I'd like to fuck you, baby, everywhere." Heat shot straight to her core; the words left her nervous, excited, and questioning. "But for tonight, I want to fuck you with that toy, if you'd like?"

The thought was hot, but worry still lingered.

"It's kind of big."

Kristina was looking down at her with so much care and so much hunger it made her head spin.

"I'll work you up to it, baby, if you want to."

She did.

She nodded.

With a wicked grin, Kristina disappeared down her body, kissing and licking and tugging at her clothes. Parker felt her socks being tugged off, the rough slide of denim down her legs, followed by the whisper of silk.

"Did I mention I missed you?"

She didn't have time to reply, before a tongue slicked hard across her, Kristina's hair soft against her thighs, and her head was back, eyes closed.

Slim fingers gripped her legs and ran up over her hips, then nails raked back down. Somewhere under the haze of pleasure, she imagined how she must look, naked from the waist down, head back, eyes closed, mouth open, panting out her need. Where once she might have been embarrassed by the image, now somehow, it only turned her on more. She let her mind wander, opening her eyes to look down at Kristina between her legs. As if she could feel the gaze, Kristina snapped her eyes up to her, and her body jumped as she was sucked hard; then Kristina wiped her mouth, and gave her a wicked smile.

"Take off your shirt?"

Parker nodded, surprised by the question, saddened by the loss as Kristina disappeared into the bathroom.

Sitting up was uncomfortable. Her body just wanted to lie there and revel. Kristina worked on the buttons on her shirt with shaky fingers—she had to stop wearing buttons around Kristina—and finally, they were done and she was tugging the material off her shoulder and struggling out of her bra.

When she looked up, Kristina was standing in the doorway to her bathroom. Parker's gaze dropped immediately to the toy sticking out from between her legs obscenely. Looking back up to her beautiful face, eyes dark, she couldn't help but laugh.

"I'm so glad this is funny to you, sweetheart."

The mattress dipped, and she didn't think Kristina was glad at all. Parker took a deep breath, still struggling with a horrible case of the giggles, as Kristina pulled her legs apart, and then Kristina was hovering over her and all the levity left the room.

Kristina moved her slim hips, and the length of the toy pressed against her.

"Not laughing anymore?"

Biting her lip, Parker shook her head. *Is this going to hurt?*

"Words."

"No, Mistress."

Kristina was magnetic, and Parker found she couldn't look away. Her hair was tussled, hanging in soft waves over her shoulder. She slicked her tongue across her bottom lip, leaving it damp, shining, and her eyes were lit with desire. She really wanted to do this.

The toy was rubbing back and forth between them, over her, and it moved slicker, easier against Parker, bumping her pleasantly.

"Are you nervous, baby?"

The care in Kristina's tone caught her off guard.

She had to clear her throat to find her voice.

"A little." She could already see the question in Kristina's eyes, and she answered automatically. "I want to. Just slow, okay?"

Panic flared in her chest when Kristina rolled off her and settled instead beside her. She pulled her close, tugging one leg up over her hip. The toy bumped her again, and Parker understood.

"Kiss me?" Kristina said.

She pressed her lips against Kristina's, letting Kristina pull her closer until they were flush together, legs tangled, the tip of the toy sinking into her.

Kristina's fingers settled over her, rubbing her, and the tinge of pain became pleasure, sending a moan spilling from between her lips.

"Is that okay?"

Kristina was looking at her, their heads on the same pillow, so close Parker could count the tiny freckles on her nose.

"Ye-ahhh...." The word became a moan as Kristina moved her slim hips forward, pushing it into her more. Kristina's pleasure was visible on her face, and Parker wondered how this felt for her. Maybe one day they could try this in reverse. The thought was oddly pleasant, and she relaxed into it, into the soft rocking of Kristina's hips building a steady rhythm inside her.

"Did you..." She couldn't finish the question.

"Only half."

That made sense. Then Kristina was kissing her, and nothing made sense. Her body burned at the intrusion between her legs, but the careful fingers that grazed her made it bearable. Kristina rocked into her, and Parker let herself get lost in touching her, kissing her, in the lips on her neck and the body flush against her own, until she was tightening, building, and she was rocking with Kristina too.

"Sweetheart..."

It was breathless, and it wasn't a command, but a plea. Parker let it spur her on, rolling her hips a little more insistently, rewarded with a soft sound of pleasure and surprise from her usually quiet lover.

Her climax was coming, building, pressing closer with every slide of fingers over her, every press of the toy that connected them inside, but more consuming was Kristina. Her breaths were short, her dark eyes fluttering closed and then resuming the fight to stay open. The fingers in Parker's hair were gentle, and when they kissed it was softer, deeper, heavier than it had ever been.

"Krissie…"

She hadn't meant to say it. Kristina's eyes snapped to her, and for a second, they were laid open, a flash of fear and so much longing that Parker closed the space between them and kissed her. She ground her hips hard against Kristina, feeling the toy move deeper inside, her body jumping at the sensation.

"Okay?"

The word was breathy, barely there, and Parker nodded, their foreheads pressed together.

"Yes, honey, just…"

Kristina held her hip, guiding her, tugging her up and closer, changing the angle, and *God*.

"I'm close too, baby."

Parker tried to cling to the words, to let them anchor her, keep her from floating away on the feelings ripping through her. Once upon a time she'd experimented with toys, but this was unlike anything she had achieved.

Soft lips pressed messy against the corner of her mouth, bringing her back to the moment, and she moved as prompted, twisting dark hair back from Kristina's cheek and watching her beautiful face. Her body burned, and she wanted her undone, as if her own climax depended on it.

"Do you like this, honey?"

Kristina nodded, her bottom lip so tight between her teeth that part of Parker worried it would bleed.

"You feel so good in me, Kristina."

Parker's body reacted directly to the moan the words elicited. She clenched hard, deliciously, confusingly full now.

"Is this what you wanted?"

She tugged softly on Kristina's hair, tilting her head back to hold her gaze, unashamed by her own stuttering breaths, the need she knew was painted all over her face.

"Yes..." The reply was a hiss, and Parker's insides quivered, the hand at her hip tightening ever so slightly as Kristina picked up the pace between them.

She opened her mouth to speak again, but she was so close, everything in her wound so tight, a moan escaped instead. Sucking in a breath, determined to see Kristina undone, she grit the words out.

"No one...has ever...had me like this. Only you...only you, honey."

Kristina's dark eyes flared, and she rocked into her harder. Parker's eyes fell closed, Kristina's slim hips flush now against her own.

"Relax, baby..."

Kristina kissed her cheek, her chin, her nose softly, and she was in control again, though the strain in her voice told Parker she was close to falling apart.

"You're mine... You're all mine, sweetheart...always...."

Parker moaned her agreement, long and loud and unashamed.

Teeth nipped her throat and her walls quivered.

Kristina was chanting in her ear over and over, and Parker had never wanted to belong to someone as much, never felt such an overwhelming sense of belonging as she did with her.

"Krissie..." It was a demand and a request, and Kristina drove into her, the hand on Parker's clit slipping away to grab at her backside and tug her forward so she met the thrust just right. She heard Kristina's breath catch, felt her tense, and then Parker was coming, long and hard, to a backdrop of Kristina moaning, shaking, jolting against her. The toy moved inside her, and it was like her pleasure was never quite done. Fingers dug into the soft flesh of her backside, teeth in the thin skin of her shoulder.

They were still moving together when she forced her eyes open. Kristina's were still closed as Parker rolled on top of her, shooting open when Parker rocked herself onto the toy insistently.

"Sweetheart."

She was breathless, beautiful as Parker struggled to find her hands and tugged them up to hold them against the pillow above her head.

She watched panic flare in Kristina's eyes, and kissed her until she felt her relax.

They fit together as easy like this as they ever had. Kristina's hips moved under her, and Parker busied herself with kissing as much of her as she could reach, tasting the sweat-slick skin of her neck, her clavicle, her shoulder.

Another orgasm was building, low in her stomach, as her hips ground into Kristina's, her nipples rubbing against her breasts, her tongue in her mouth.

"Parker..."

Parker pulled back and looked down at her, lips swollen, parted, eyes dark, hungry, open, her hands still clasped above her head.

She was in love with Kristina.

"Okay?"

Kristina nodded, and Parker sank back down to kiss her. She forced herself to rock faster, harder, her thighs tensed tight, ignoring her own pleasure until Kristina's body bowed off the bed, and she keened, long and high. Kristina shuddered below her, and strong hands pulled her down, tugging her forward and letting the toy push into her at just the right angle to shove her over the edge.

"Sweetheart..."

Parker lost herself in that voice, in the arms around her, the body under her. Kristina held her there, rolling her hips softly, slowly, until Parker was limp above her, spent.

Finally, the arms holding her loosened, and she rolled as she was prompted, jumping uncomfortably as the thing slipped from inside her. A thud sounded in the quiet room and she guessed Kristina had tossed it aside, and then she was back, half on top of her. Parker wrapped her arms around her without thinking.

"Sleep?"

She was already drifting.

Chapter Fifteen

"EXCUSE ME, PROFESSOR."

Kristina appeared in the bathroom doorway, hair still wet from the shower, pajama pants and a T-shirt hanging loose from her small frame.

Parker tugged her glasses off her nose and set her phone aside—student emails could wait, definitely.

"Oh no, please, keep those on."

She sauntered across the room, and Parker watched, spellbound, wondering if she would ever get tired of this woman. Even after last night when they were both thoroughly sated, desire crackled between them again like a static charge, though it was gentler now than it had been at the start.

The mattress dipped as Kristina sat beside her, and she studiously ignored the way her heart jumped when Kristina leaned in to kiss her.

"So you're in a better mood this morning?" Parker asked the question against soft lips.

"I recall being in an awfully good mood last night."

Parker nipped at the tongue that was playing at her lips.

"If that's my punishment, I may have to make you jealous more often, Miss Diaz."

Kristina stiffened under her touch.

"It's nothing to be ashamed of."

Dark hair fell in Kristina's face as she looked down, and reaching up to twist it back over her shoulder had become so natural Parker did it without even thinking.

"Krissie, it's natural. We all experience it at some point in our lives."

The nickname earned her a kiss.

"Not for me. I don't do jealousy, as a rule. I don't tolerate it from my subs, and I seriously never engage in it."

"Why?"

She searched Kristina's eyes, trying to follow where she had gone again. The place was far, and cold, and everything was so clear-cut that Parker didn't understand it at all.

"Because it's just insecurity given airtime. We live in an amazing world; there's so much to experience. If I interact with someone else, it doesn't change how I feel about you. I think it's crazy to believe you can be absolutely everything to someone else, and it's selfish to expect it."

Wow.

"So you're polyamorous?"

"What? No." Kristina's eyebrows shot up. "That implies I have feelings for multiple people. I don't."

"You just want to sleep with multiple people?"

She wished she hadn't said it. As soon as it left her mouth, her own jealousy stirred. Maybe she was selfish, but the thought of Kristina with someone else twisted something deep in her gut.

"Lately, no."

The admission felt huge in the quiet of the room.

"Kristina... There won't be any more dates. I mean, I'm not planning on doing that again."

Somehow it felt important to say. Kristina's eyes were on her, full of apology and a thousand questions. She asked one of her own.

"Are we...being exclusive?"

Her heart beat harder at the suggestion. Experience had taught her that Kristina would balk at the commitment, but hope made her ask anyway.

"Parker... I..." She paused, running a hand through wet hair, beautiful in the late-morning sun peeling in through the windows. "I want to say yes, and that terrifies me. This isn't who I am."

Parker's heart soared and then stuttered, but for now, it was enough.

"So don't say anything."

Maybe she was wrong to keep giving her all these concessions and ways out, and she could only imagine what Marion would say, but against all the odds, she trusted Kristina. As much as her reasoning was lost on her, and as much as she didn't understand the invisible and ever-changing standard she seemed to hold herself to, Parker knew without a doubt Kristina wasn't out to hurt her.

Kristina picked at a thread on her pants, goose bumps on the tops of her arms from the cool of the room after her shower. She'd never wanted anything like this, like her.

"Planning on going out to do your yoga this morning?"

Seemingly relieved by the change of subject, Kristina flopped back onto the pillows beside her, and Parker tried to ignore how natural it was to lean down and kiss her. When she pulled back, Kristina's eyes were shining up at her with their usual mirth.

"Not unless you want to join me?"

Parker laughed.

"And humiliate myself, flailing around while you fold yourself like a pretzel?"

"Oh..."

Kristina caught her by the shirt and tugged her back down. She went easily.

"So you do watch me."

Her cheeks did flame a little bit at that. It had become a guilty pleasure, lying in bed looking out of the window to watch the sunrise over the ocean and ogle Kristina in those *oh so thin* spandex pants.

"What if I do?"

A smirk lit her beautiful face.

"I know what I'm getting you for Christmas then."

Somehow, the permanence in the words surprised her. It was the most Kristina had ever talked about, or implied there would be, any future for them together. She tried not to cling to it.

The doorbell rang before she could ask what. Kristina groaned.

"Need to get that?" Parker let her fingers walk up a pajama-clad thigh, catch the hem of her shirt, and tug it up to expose a thin sliver of skin above her waistband. She raked her nails over it softly.

"I don't want to." Kristina shivered under the touch. "But I should."

Parker kissed her, slow and deep, and just when Kristina's fingers came up to thread through her hair, she pulled back.

"Go ahead, honey. I'll be here."

She huffed out a sigh.

"You're evil, Professor, but I'll have the last laugh."

Parker picked up her phone as she rolled away. She slipped her glasses back onto her nose, looking over the rims as the doorbell rang again.

"I'm counting on it. Now go answer the door."

With one last scorching look, Kristina disappeared down the hall.

The sound of voices floated up to meet her. Focusing on her emails, she tried not to listen, but as they grew quieter, discomfort settled over her.

Conscious she was prying but concerned, she set her phone aside, left her glasses on the nightstand, and started down the long hall after Kristina.

Voices rose—she could make out Kristina's and another woman's—until she was hovering outside the living room door.

"I told you, I'm busy."

Kristina sounded as fraught as she'd ever heard her, and Parker entered the room without thinking. The woman from that day in the driveway was there. Her dark eyes snapped to her, all lithe feline grace as she stepped easily around Kristina to move toward her.

"A sleepover? TPE round the clock?"

Lost, Parker opened her mouth to ask what she meant, but Kristina was at her side, half between her and the woman who Parker knew by now to be Mal.

"No. Can we do this some other time?"

Mal didn't seem to hear her.

"Older. I'm impressed. I can work with this."

Parker felt herself being appraised and squared her shoulders, wishing she was wearing something other than sweats and an old T-shirt, wishing she was wearing a bra.

"Mallory Carlson."

"Parker Freeman." She held Mal's gaze, feeling Kristina beside her, tense, watching the interaction.

"So, Parker. Kristina and I were going to play. I'd be happy to have you join. It would be good for you to spend time with a more experienced Dominant."

It took her a second to realize what she meant. Kristina was oddly quiet, still at her side, so unlike the confident, carefree woman she usually was in front of anyone else.

"Actually, it sounded like Kristina asked you to leave."

Mal's smile twisted into something sinister, and she laughed. The sound was rough, and the chill it sent down Parker's spine was anything but pleasant.

"Fiery. I see why she likes you." She seemed to consider for a second, and Parker held her gaze. "You can join us, or leave. Which will it be?"

Is she for real? Kristina went to speak, but Parker was faster.

"What exactly will I be joining you in? Has Kristina said she wants to have sex with you, or be dominated by you, or whatever you're hoping is going to happen here?"

The scent of perfume assaulted her as Mal stepped into her space. They were close enough to kiss, but against all her instinct, Parker didn't step back.

"Kristina is mine."

"Honey." Parker forced herself to look away from Mal, to Kristina who looked small, lost, beside her, watching the interaction between the two of them intensely. Mal scoffed at the endearment. "Do you want me to leave? Do you want to..." She couldn't bring herself to call it *playing*. "Be with her?"

"Of course she does. Isn't that right, pet?"

Mal answered for her, and Kristina swallowed hard, dark eyes falling to the floor, silent. That was no kind of answer.

"You need to leave."

If Kristina wanted her to go she could say so, but until then, Parker wasn't leaving her alone with this woman. Mal licked her lips and stepped impossibly closer.

Mal reached up. Parker swallowed hard as she waited for Mal's fingers to brush her cheek. They never made contact.

Suddenly awake, moving, Kristina was between them, conviction burning in her voice.

"Don't touch her."

Mal laughed, and Parker was lost, missing too many vital pieces to make real sense of this interaction. The fingers of Kristina's free hand shook at her side, and it was so natural to step up to her back and slide her own through them, squeezing gently.

"Kristina..."

Mal pulled her arm from her grip, roughly.

"Just leave. I've told you, I don't want you here anymore."

Mal's nostrils flared. Her gaze on Kristina was scorching, even as a bystander.

"Why? Because of her?"

Parker opened her mouth to tell her it was none of her business, but Mal spoke again.

"You will always, always be a broken little girl, Kristina. You might enjoy playing Mistress, but you and I, we know the truth of what you are. And you *will* come back to me."

It sounded too much like a threat. Kristina's fingers shook in her own, and Parker stepped closer, her other hand soft on her hip as she addressed Mal.

"You need to leave."

Mal snapped her eyes to her, studying her, analyzing her with such contempt, such condescension, that it was an effort not to wilt under her glare. Parker's front pressed soft against Kristina's back. Parker let her presence fortify her, inflate her. She had something Mal didn't. Kristina was hers, for now.

"You heard her." Kristina took a shuddering breath. "Get the fuck out, Mal, and don't come back. It's over between us, it has been for a while, and I mean it, I'm done."

Mal's face was sour as she took a step away, and as Kristina relaxed against her, Parker felt like, finally, it was safe to exhale.

A sound rang out like a gunshot, too fast, out of absolutely nowhere, and Mal sprung forward. Kristina let out a strangled cry and jumped back covering her face, colliding into Parker who wrapped her arms around her without thinking.

The room was silent, and it took Parker three long seconds to realize the noise had just been the stomp of Mal's stiletto on the floor. The action made no sense, but Kristina was shaking against her, and Mal was laughing, cold, callous. *Did she pretend to hit her?*

"I'll be seeing you, K."

Thankfully, she did turn to leave, and Parker waited, listening to the click of her heels down the hall, the open and close of the front door, the roar of her car speeding out of the driveway.

Kristina's breathing was ragged, uneven in the quiet.

"What just happened?"

Kristina made no move to answer, still clinging to her, small, quiet, in a way Parker had never seen her.

"Krissie?"

Taking hold of Kristina's biceps, she tried to move her away, but Kristina held tight, and unsure what else to do, Parker walked them to the sofa and sat them down.

Kristina's slim arms were tight around her waist, so Parker let them stay, keeping her own around her, holding her close, running her fingers through her silky dark hair.

The interaction replayed in her mind. She studied it from every angle. Most of it she could make some sense of, but the last part, Mal's stiletto on the floor, Kristina's reaction and the hand over her face... *Did she hit her when they were together?*

"Sorry...I..." Kristina pulled back, and Parker let her go just enough so she could see her face, still holding her gently around the arms. "You shouldn't have had to see that."

She dragged her thumbs under Kristina's eyes, collecting the last of the tears, and Parker found herself struck by how young she looked, how small, in comparison to the force of nature she had become to her.

"You have nothing to apologize for, honey, nothing."

Kristina nodded, blinking at her before her face clouded over.

"I should... You should..."

"Kristina, did she hit you?"

She hadn't meant to just come out with it, but watching the mask fall back into place, seeing Kristina preparing to run, she had.

"Mal?" The word was sputtered out, and more tears welled in her dark eyes.

Parker tipped her head.

"No... Never. Mal... She's just... God."

The tears spilled over, and Kristina's face disappeared into her hands. Parker tugged her closer, and though she resisted at first, eventually, she collapsed against her chest again.

"Is this why you were so upset the last time she was here?"

Kristina nodded against her.

"I wasn't having work done at the house. I just wanted not to be here because I knew she was in town. She got here early," she said darkly. Parker sensed her hackles rising.

"Krissie... If she's been hurting you...."

Kristina pulled away from her. "No, Parker, no. Mal has never hurt me without my consent."

"Has she fucked you without it?"

The silence that hung between them was loaded and heavy, and stretched out too long. As she opened her mouth to break it, Kristina spoke.

"No... I don't know. It's over now, so what does it matter?"

"Kristina..."

"Parker, please." She sounded just desperate, just broken enough that Parker let her protests die on her tongue, and they hovered there, both caught in heavy silence.

Parker reached across the space that had sprung up between them and then she took Kristina's cool fingers in her own, squeezing, tugging a little, until Kristina was looking up at her, a fresh wave of tears in her dark eyes though her mouth stayed set in a grim line.

"I'm sorry. I'm just trying to understand this...you. I...care about you."

Kristina swallowed hard.

"I know."

"How did this become your life, Krissie? You're so…. Good, you have so much potential. What made you use the agency and go with Mal?"

She scoffed.

"You used the agency too."

Parker nodded her agreement. "And I'm a forty-year-old woman whose entire life flipped when my wife left me and I was desperate to get out of that…place, to find myself again, that I figured I had nothing to lose, but you…"

"Don't." Kristina's voice was sharp as broken glass. "Don't put me up on a pedestal." Tears tracked down her cheeks.

"Krissie…"

Parker leaned in, not knowing what to do. Sex was always easy between them, and physically, they communicated on a level she didn't know how to replicate with words in that moment. Hovering a hairsbreadth away from her, she waited, Kristina exhaling against her lips. When she leaned forward to press their mouths together, it was soft, slow. Parker reached up to cup her face, tears collecting on her thumbs.

When the kiss ended, they stayed close, foreheads resting together as she brushed the tears from Kristina's tan cheeks.

I love you.

The words rang in her head, screamed. She did. Somehow, somewhere in all this she had fallen for Kristina, and all she wanted was to protect her, to understand her, to help her heal. The way she'd flinched back haunted Parker as much as the words, but she gave in to the silence, closing her eyes to enjoy Kristina's proximity, the fact that for now, she was hers.

"I got into a bad relationship coming out of high school. It messed me up more than I can tell you. He, um..."

Parker watched her as she pulled away, trying not to feel the slight shock that ran through her at the pronoun.

"He hit me, and was controlling, and...I was young."

A sob rattled up her throat, but when Parker reached for her, Kristina held up her hands.

"If you touch me, I won't be able to finish. I've not told anyone this in years."

Parker nodded her understanding, trying desperately to keep her emotions off her face as she folded her hands back in her lap and listened.

"Afterwards I just... I was so out of control. I called the agency when I was twenty and met Mal shortly after. I hated her at first, but over time she showed me intimacy I understood. Like a business transaction, the terms are set. I understood the stakes for both parties, and what she got, and what I got, and there was a get-out clause from the start."

Parker swallowed, tears welling as Kristina reached up to wipe hers away.

"Mal was good to me. I found it hard to say no to her even when our arrangement ended, and after I met you I...asked her to stop coming around; then I started trying to avoid her. She fixed me, or I thought she had, and now I just..."

Her face crumpled. Parker caught her without hesitation when she leaned forward to sob, held her until she'd taken a deep breath, and met her eyes again.

"I had it all figured out." The words were soft in the quiet, still a little unsteady. Kristina's dark eyes met her own, and something constricted in her chest. "I never knew until you that nothing was figured out at all."

It shattered. Kristina leaned up as she leaned down, and they were kissing, soft but firm. Kristina ran her fingers over Parker's shirt, up her chest to touch her neck, her cheeks, her hair.

Those three words she really didn't want to say were right on the tip of her tongue, so she put it to better use by running it soft across Kristina's bottom lip and letting it flit inside. Parker had never tasted her like this, laid open, the last of her defenses blown out with the admission neither of them had expected.

The pads of Kristina's fingers trailed down her spine, settled on her hip. Parker tugged her closer, closer, and there was no trace of dominant Kristina as lips moved to kiss the hollow of her throat.

Clothes fell like rain, and when they tumbled back onto the sofa, the softness stayed. Kristina looked up at her, and Parker saw her eyes question and then let go, give in when she touched her gently.

I love you.

It was right there, so she dipped her head instead. She kissed Kristina and let the word fall out silently into her mouth.

Her name sounded like a benediction, falling from kiss-plumped lips as she moved down her body. Though she had seen her countless times, everything looked different today in the face of this new exposition between them. It was with one hand on Kristina's cheek, and her lips around a taut nipple that Parker realized what was happening.

"Parker..."

Her name had never sounded as good, as right, as it did in that moment when Kristina breathed it out and let her head fall back on the cushion.

It had never sounded as good as when Parker slid back up to slip a thigh between her legs and kiss her slowly. Fingers threaded through her hair, holding her impossibly closer. They didn't twist or tug. There was no play for the upper hand; there were no games at all now. Kristina was relaxed against her as Parker slid a hand between them, relaxed when Kristina bucked her hips and pushed her half off so she could slide her own hand down too. They touched each other slowly, unhurried, soft moans and breathy gasps and Kristina's body shuddering in a way that made her ache.

"Krissie..."

Kristina's fingers moved slick over her, and Parker tried for focus on moving her own against Kristina, on her half-lidded eyes and barely parted lips, on anything except the words bubbling so close to the surface, threatening to spill out and ruin whatever tentative thing was forming between them now.

Parker had seen her naked, been undone by her dozens of times, yet somehow, this felt like the first time Kristina was truly bare before her.

"Krissie..."

The words rose higher, closer, and it would be so easy to let them fall out on a breath, spill them out into the day where so many other admissions had been made anyway.

There was a warning in Kristina's eyes, and Parker slid her fingers lower, pushing into her slowly, almost apologetic; then her jaw was clenched and the words were tumbling away. If she couldn't tell, she would show her.

Parker didn't ask permission this time, letting the tips of her fingers dip low, feeling Kristina tense beneath her, feeling the hitch in her kiss before she relaxed, her hips rising ever so slightly, inviting. Parker pushed into her.

Parker didn't stop. She didn't even falter when somewhere between the slide of their bodies, the throbbing pleasure that was winding higher from having Kristina inside her, against her, on her, she realized they weren't fucking. She had never dared to touch her like this, with such reverence, so lazily. Kristina had always been something to be enjoyed quickly and thoroughly, taking as much as she dared before she pulled away. Today, there was no rush, no games, or roles, or *yes, Mistress*. They were making love.

Parker dipped her head and kissed a trail, messy up Kristina's throat, dark hair spilling over her shoulders, sticking to her lips. Head back, eyes closed, short breaths whistling between her lips, Kristina let her.

"Sweetheart..."

Parker was close, her body as tight, as desperate as she had ever been for her, even without all Kristina's usual clever demands. Looking down at her, somewhere through the haze, through the orgasm building hot and hard to contain in her stomach, Parker told herself to save this moment. Kristina watched her, tan cheeks flushed, full lips wrapped around her name.

Fingers curled inside her, and she twisted her own in response, feeling herself cresting but determined to take Kristina with her. Collapsing forward to kiss her, she pushed her thumb against her harder, elated and relieved when Kristina clenched and then fluttered around her fingers and they were falling apart together.

Parker was in love with her.

Soft fingers held her close, while defter ones curled inside her, drawing out her orgasm.

Somewhere in all this, she had fallen for Kristina. Beyond wanting more, she just wanted her.

Parker sucked in a breath, her head on Kristina's shoulder as she moved her own hand slightly, tugging the last bits of pleasure from the woman beneath her, enjoying feeling her like this.

Kristina jumped when Parker slipped out of her, and Parker heard her own soft noise when she did the same. Then they were silent, whatever had settled over them still unbroken even with their orgasms done. She traced careful patterns over Kristina's collarbone with her nail, felt the play of fingers lazy in her hair. Part of her was holding her breath, waiting for it all to crash, for Kristina to tense, to slip out of her embrace, to run as she always had in the past when they had danced too close to this line. Now they had danced right across it.

"What are you thinking about?"

The words surprised her, and she shook her head, too afraid to shatter this moment.

"Parker..." It was half a request, half more, soft and reassuring, and she sighed.

"I used to think I had everything so figured out and I knew myself so well and knew what I wanted. Like I set my life on this path, and closed my eyes to everything but following it and clinging to it. I was a passenger, and that was fine with me. I never knew there was another option, until you."

Kristina surprised her with a kiss.

"I did tell you you would have all the control, all the power."

This time it was Parker who leaned up to kiss her.

"In that case, will you accompany me to bed?"

Something fluttered in her stomach at her own boldness, her brazenness, sweat still drying on the back of her neck from their last round of lovemaking, yet she was unashamed now she wanted more.

"Look at you."

Kristina leaned up and kissed her, and Parker tasted pride on her lips. Together they were better, so much more, and suddenly the future felt tangible, and close, and like something they could maybe achieve together.

Kristina pulled back, breathless, and licked her lips.

"Lead the way."

Chapter Sixteen

KRISTINA WAS AWAKE, already above the covers. Parker felt her eyes on her as she blinked through the first light of the sun breaking the horizon.

"Morning?"

Kristina nodded, and when Parker reached for her, she stiffened. The warm glow Parker had fallen asleep to, the replay of last night that had woken her, shattered.

"Everything okay?"

Kristina collected herself enough to smile through the dim light, to squeeze the fingers that had caught her knee, but Parker knew.

"Of course. I just couldn't sleep."

Cold settled into her bones.

"I have an early meeting, some execs from out of town, they fly out tonight so..."

And like that, she was being dismissed again, but not just for the day. Parker felt Kristina pulling back, untangling the pieces of them that had become so irreversibly knotted together over the past six months. She knew without hearing the words. She had tried to fly, and they had fallen. All that was left to do was meet the ground.

"Kristina."

She didn't want to pretend, to wait, to feel it coming. God, she wasn't ready to lose her.

"I have to go get dressed."

When lips pressed against hers they were quick, barely there before they were gone. She tried too hard to understand why Kristina had kissed her at all, when kisses were something that had never been expected, as much as they'd been a nice surprise, before.

Stumbling through getting dressed, choking on all the tears she was holding in her throat, Parker heard Marion's words over and over.

She was always meant to be temporary.

Foolishly she had thought maybe together they could find something permanent. Stupid. Another bad decision, another huge bout of misplaced faith. She'd thought maybe for her, Kristina would change her mind, maybe she could be the exception.

"I made you coffee."

They knew. It hung between them and Parker just wanted to scream it, and she wanted to bury it, to knock the coffee out of her hand and let it splash all over the smooth floor of the foyer and kiss her until they could forget. She was frozen.

"Sweetheart?"

Hope glittered in her chest, dangerous, but the regret, the remorse in Kristina's eyes following the endearment, crushed it.

"Right. I can eat at home, if you need to go?"

Kristina nodded gratefully, and Parker followed her to the garage. Horribly, achingly aware this was the last time she would see the house, the last time she would be in her space. This was the last time she would get into this car.

"Parker."

Kristina was holding the door for her as she always did, eyes hidden. Parker wondered if she would survive this car ride, and not because of Kristina's driving.

It passed too quickly, a blur of quiet Saturday morning streets. Somehow this hurt, burrowed inside her more than her divorce ever had. Being served the papers was embarrassing; it set her drifting, loosed her from the life she thought she had somehow earned by staying and staying and staying. Losing Amanda, losing the life she'd always planned for herself never quite derailed her, never quite broke her like the distance between them as Kristina's hands sat white-knuckled on the steering wheel just feet away. Why couldn't Parker just have been her...submissive? Why did she have to fall in love? Why couldn't Kristina just fucking love her back?

"Need help with your bag?"

It was barely an overnight bag, not heavy at all, and the question seemed strange. Parker looked up at her house, trying to blink the tears out of her eyes, trying not to imagine all the nights she would spend inside replaying what she knew was going to come next, missing her.

"Just say it, Kristina."

She couldn't even look at her.

"What—"

"Don't. Don't lie to me."

She heard her swallow, heard the click of her seat belt releasing, but Parker didn't move. Seconds ticked fast and slow, and all the hurt in her chest twisted, and she was angry, bleeding, and oh so tired. She turned to Kristina, because fuck it all, the end was going to come with or without her and she was done being a spectator in her own life.

"Isn't this the part where you end it respectfully? Time to move on, right? Find a new sub. Someone who won't cross your lines like I did?"

Face ashen, Kristina blinked at her, before she looked away, letting out a long breath through her nose.

"Parker... I..." She swallowed hard, and stupid, traitorous hope burst in Parker's chest again. This had never been her. She'd never been the woman who thought she could beat all the odds, who believed in fairy tales, who ran off and entered into some BDSM relationship with a woman half her age. She was the woman who worked hard for what she had, who stuck to the path, who kept her eyes closed and walked on. Yet she wanted it. She wanted Kristina to cry and give in and embrace what they had. She wanted to be the one she changed for; she wanted to be her exception.

"I can't do relationships."

The end.

Part of her was calm, and part of her raged. She was the eye of the storm, one foot in the twister, one foot outside, and nothing had ever hurt like this.

"You can, because you did. We did it all, Kristina, relationships, feelings and...love, and it was wonderful. So you *can*; you are capable." Everything inside her told her to give up, to walk away.

"If you don't want to; if this is because of your ex or Mal..."

Kristina's eyes were set hard, and she was beautiful, even at the end. Parker could still see past the mask, and Kristina looked haunted.

"This is because of me, because of who I am and the kind of life I want to live."

The blow landed with a finality that stole Parker's breath.

"A life without me."

She was already nodding, accepting the words, letting them sink into her psyche, propel her forward until she was unbuckling her seat belt and throwing open the door.

Tears dripped pitifully down her cheeks. *God, how did I let myself want this?* She didn't know herself as she rose from the car. She didn't know the woman who was happy to be divorced, who enjoyed being tied up and called a *good girl*, the woman who fell in love with someone half her age and ached down to her bones to run headlong into another forever with her. She was practical Parker, Parker who *had stayed*, Parker whose life fit her mold, right up until she was wide-awake Parker, madly in love with the most emotionally unavailable woman she had ever met. She didn't know which was real.

"Goodbye, Kristina."

She couldn't turn back. She didn't trust herself to look at her, not to give in and round the car and make all of this go away. Part of her thought she could. Kristina had taught her about life, love, and she had taught her sex could be a weapon. She could drop her bag and crawl across the console, throw the match on the gasoline, and use that weapon one more time.

"I never meant to fall in love with you."

Parker spun around. Her heart beat hard and then it stopped. *Kristina fell in love with me.* It should be everything she'd ever wanted to hear, but now, staring down the end, it only hurt more.

Kristina's eyes were on hers, and Parker promised herself just three seconds, three more seconds to look at her, to let those words wash over her and through her and raise her high and drown her deeper. Kristina swallowed, and the countdown was done.

"Goodbye, Parker."

Twin tears spilled down her tan cheeks, and Parker couldn't look anymore.

Turning back to her driveway and starting down it in long determined steps, she heard the squeal of tires on the street. Then Kristina was gone.

Chapter Seventeen

THE COMMUNITY CENTER loomed up ahead, and Marion bumped her hip softly.

"So have you heard from her at all?"

Parker shot her a look. It had been weeks, almost a month since that morning outside her house, almost a month of deafening radio silence.

"No, and I'm not going to. That's just how it is…"

She felt Marion's eyes on her, and she ignored them, carrying on at their glacial pace down the street, roped into baby class with her best friend while LiLing had to work.

"Parker, you cried more over her than you ever did over Amanda, more than I've ever seen you."

Something inside her that had been coiled tight since the first mention of…her broke.

"Well, you weren't supposed to see any of it, but you practically broke in so…"

She didn't mean to snap, but she didn't want to talk about it, or think about it, not anymore.

"Hey."

Marion stopped abruptly and dragged her to a halt by the elbow, forcing the pedestrians behind them to swerve to avoid hitting them. The spring sun was pleasant on her cheeks, the back of her neck beneath her ponytail. The workout pants she wore were tighter than they might have been *pre-her*, the shirt a little more revealing, the thin straps of her sports bra crisscrossed over her half-bare back. Kristina was gone, but the changes she had brokered lingered.

"I'm worried about you." Marion's eyes bored into her. "Sure, you're not crying anymore, and you're not online reading those horrific forum board things anymore, but you're...like a cyborg."

Parker spun on her heel and redoubled her pace toward the doors to the building, leaving her friend to waddle to catch up.

"P...Parker...Parker Elise, so help me, if I have this baby early while running after you..."

She skidded to another stop, huffing out a breath.

"Do you want me to apologize because I'm not broken up over this?" *I am broken up over it.* There were a hundred tiny, sharp pieces inside her chest that twisted and tore and poked at her at least five times a day still, but dwelling on them didn't serve her at all.

"I didn't mean that. I'm sorry." Marion was puffing, catching her breath, and Parker couldn't help but feel guilty.

"You know I love you. It's just so unlike you. You're all work and this strange efficiency and new confidence and—"

Parker raised her eyebrows. "Seriously, M, put down the shovel."

"I'm sorry, I'm sorry!" Her best friend pressed a hand to her brow. "These third trimester hormones are just... My brain and mouth aren't on speaking terms." She took a deep breath and seemed to clear her head. "Are you happy?"

Parker sighed.

"We're going to be late." Couples were passing them now, heading through the doors.

"Parker..."

Marion grabbed her hand, keeping her from turning and following them.

"No... But I will be." Parker squeezed the fingers in her own with all the conviction she could muster. "Now come on, Lily's going to be pissed if we don't record the entire class this time."

Marion's eyes held hers for a few seconds longer, and thankfully, she seemed to relent.

"It's not like we haven't already been through this once with Roland... I get it, she's an over-preparer, but if I have to do another role-play I swear to—"

Parker thanked the man holding the door for them loudly enough to cut off her ranting, and pushed her along by the shoulders toward the meeting room where the class would be held.

Twenty minutes later Marion was perched on a blue rubber ball, Parker's hands on her shoulders while they were supposed to be role-playing positive encouragement techniques.

"You turned on the recorder, right... For Lily?"

Parker patted her shoulder, eyes moving through the room, from the obnoxious instructor to couple after couple, most of them a man and a woman, though she was pleased to spot two men and another all-woman duo too.

"Yes. Keep breathing; you're doing great. The pain is temporary, and you survived this once already, though your lady bits will never be the same, you're creating new life, etcetera."

Marion laughed long and loud, earning them a glare from the instructor, before they both dipped their heads.

"Thank you for doing this."

There was softness in Marion's voice she hadn't expected. There had been a distance between them since things ended with *her*, and Parker knew she was the one who had put it there.

"Of course, M. How could I not want to do this with you? I'm so excited for you guys. You know that, right?"

Marion nodded so quickly she almost unbalanced herself on the ball, her prominent stomach pushing her center of gravity off. Parker held her steady, smiling down at the grateful look she received in thanks.

"It's just—I know once upon a time you really wanted all this. The wife and the kids and..." Her pity turned to curiosity, and Parker preferred it. "Do you still?"

Do I?

"I think..."

The instructor passed by and she mumbled a few encouragements, and Marion breathed emphatically, halfway to flipping the woman the bird after she passed before Parker could slap her hand down.

"Honestly, I don't know."

Marion bounced lightly on her ball. Tired of hovering behind her, Parker plopped down on the mat beside her, holding her ankle in a show of faux support.

"I think more than I actually wanted all that, I just wanted a life that fit, that was expected and known. Like with Amanda, I was just so desperate to be..."

She waved her hands, and Marion nodded her understanding without her having to find the elusive word, urging her on.

"I just set myself on this path, and it was only after clinging to it so hard, then losing it all that I realized how poorly it fit me. I wanted the wife and the kids and the big house, sure, but I think what I really wanted was just to belong, for things to feel permanent." She swallowed and had to look away, glancing around the room instead of looking into those brown eyes she knew would see her soul.

"Now, after everything, I think maybe it's less important for everything to fit neatly into that mold than it is just to find that connection, find someone who makes me the best version of myself, and celebrates me for what I am instead of being so hung up on this idea of perfect that really wouldn't have been, if Amanda and I had done it."

She flicked her gaze back to Marion's face, her wariness at what she might find there melting at the tears in her best friend's eyes.

"Sorry, sorry... It's the hormones." Marion dabbed her eyes with a sleeve. "You really loved her."

This time it wasn't a question. Parker had. Somewhere amongst it all, the thrill of it, and the impossibility, the unconventionality, they had hit a rhythm and the beat was easy, and Parker had danced, totally unapologetically herself, for the first time in her life.

"I did."

She swallowed the tears in her throat.

"Can't you call her?"

The question was tentative, careful now as it hadn't been the millions of times it had been asked over the last month.

Parker sighed out a breath.

"She doesn't want a relationship, and as much as I want to pretend I could handle going back to just...our arrangement." She paused to glance warily around the room, relieved no one seemed to be listening. "I can't. We can't uncross that line, and I can't make her be in a relationship she doesn't want... I don't want to."

She picked at a loose thread on Marion's super stretchy yoga pants.

"I deserve better than someone who doesn't want to be with me, really be with me, all of me. She taught me that." The last part was a sad admission, and a fresh wave of tears welled up in Marion's eyes, a few falling down her cheeks before she swiped at them and apologized again. Parker patted her calf, surprised by the strength in her own voice.

"It's okay."

It wasn't. None of it was okay. She missed Kristina terribly, horribly, yet now she was herself, the self she had lost for so many years, and she clung to that like a life raft.

"What are you going to do?"

She swallowed hard, sucking in a breath and raising her chin ever so slightly, offering a smile she hoped would reassure them both.

"I'm going to get on with my life."

MISS BRENNA CARL was everything she had expected Kristina to be, a stern brunette about her age, who dressed a little too ostentatiously and was forward with her in a way that made Parker uncomfortable.

Despite Marion's watchful glances and gentle disagreement, she had decided to dip her toes back into the world of kink one more time, to see what she might find there. Kristina was exactly as unique as Parker had known she would be, and judging by her meeting with Miss Carl, kink was not going to save her, or even be for her, a second time.

"So you're an experienced submissive?"

Miss Carl's blue eyes studied her, shrewd and hungry, and Parker lifted her chin and rose under the scrutiny where she once would have wilted.

"I had one ten-month relationship of that nature, yes."

Amusement creased the corner of Miss Carl's lips.

"Any hard limits?"

With Kristina there had never really been hard limits; there had been trust and mutual attraction that they had built something beautiful and functional on so effortlessly.

"Why don't we talk about your kinks?"

Miss Carl's eyes turned to blue fire at her defiance.

"Tell me about yourself then?" she offered instead. "Why did your last relationship end? What are you looking for here?"

At least she referred to it as a relationship. Parker couldn't help but make a note that was at least one step up from Kristina, even if everything else set her teeth on edge.

"My last relationship ended because we were no longer compatible." The words tumbled out like they were read from a script. Sure, trust and honesty were important in a relationship like this, but somehow, she didn't want to bare her soul to this woman. Honestly, she didn't want to bare her anything right now and wasn't sure she ever would.

"I'm an English professor at a local school, so discretion is important. I'm not looking to mix my personal life and my sex life." She arched an eyebrow until Miss Carl nodded, still watching her, a look on her face Parker struggled to decipher.

"After going through a difficult period in my life I met K... my previous—" *Girlfriend? Lover? Dominant?* "—partner, and through exploring this I regained a lot of my sense of self and my confidence." She wet her dry lips and forced herself to be brave. It was always awkward at first. She needed to give things a chance. "I'm hoping to find someone to continue that exploration with."

Brenna rose to her feet and left the room abruptly. She was gone just long enough that Parker started to wonder what she had said and if she was coming back.

When she returned, a decanter of something clasped in one hand and two crystal glasses in the other, her eyes were two shades darker.

"Call me presumptuous, but sounds like the occasion calls for a drink. I think we'll do just fine together, Parker."

Her name sounded wrong from Brenna's mouth, too high, too nasally, but she forced a smile onto her face and accepted the glass of whiskey... It was three o'clock in the afternoon and she was driving home. Kristina would never be so careless with her. The thought was enough to encourage a hearty sip down her throat. It burned pleasantly, taking the memory of Kristina with it.

"I'd like to see you, Parker."

Her eyes snapped up to Brenna's face, and just as she opened her mouth to ask what she meant, Brenna crooked an index finger.

"Stand up and take off your dress. You're a beautiful woman."

The compliment was like an afterthought; it felt like fan-service, a way to ensure she got what she wanted. Parker stood anyway. She set her drink on the coffee table between them and met those blue eyes as she lifted the hem of her dress slowly, keeping the table between them.

Her hair tickled as it fell down around her bare shoulders, and she was glad for the soft lilac lingerie she had chosen, not for Brenna, but for herself. Brenna purred appreciatively as she ran her hands down her waist, over the flat plane of her stomach that was tight now, toned, her body in the best condition it had seen in the last fifteen years.

"Turn around."

She spun slowly, looking back over her shoulder to watch greedy blue eyes trail up the back of her legs, lingering on her backside before they ascended higher still and caught her gaze.

"When we play together—" The words were deliberately slow. Maybe it was supposed to be sexy? It was just awkward, annoying, having to hold Brenna's gaze while she drawled them out. "—I'd like you to call me Mommy."

A snort of laughter escaped without her permission. Brenna crossed the room slowly, still searching for eye contact while Parker kept the tips of her fingers pressed to her mouth, her cheeks burning. She couldn't call her that.

"Do you want to be spanked, little girl?"

God, that turned her stomach, and not in a good way.

"I, uh." Her heart beat faster as Brenna stepped into her space to take her wrist and tug her fingers away from her mouth. It wasn't the rush of anticipation, excitement, Kristina had always bought. It was a frantic nervousness, a shyness, disbelief at the situation, and embarrassment at needing to find a way out of it.

"Come sit on Mommy's lap, and we'll talk about your poor behavior."

Brenna was deep in character already, and Parker dug in her heels and she was dragged back to the sofa.

"Actually, I, uh..."

"Mommy didn't ask you to speak."

Brenna's blue eyes were on her brown ones, and this was spiraling too fast.

"Okay... Red or consider this me safe wording."

Brenna paused, though the vise grip on her wrist didn't loosen like it was supposed to, the scene didn't stop completely like it should, and Parker felt the first flutters of fear in her stomach.

"In my usual arrangements, when the sub safe words, which is rarely, I assess the scene and decide if we should continue."

Parker tried to yank her hand away again, but Brenna held fast.

"That's not going to work for me."

"Why?"

Brenna stepped into her space, and she wished for her dress, wished for a way through this and around this. How the hell had she ever thought anyone else could be like Kristina to her?

"Because for me, all this hinges on trust, and if I don't trust you to respect my limits, then it's not going to work. I'm sorry."

She tacked on the apology as an afterthought, finally tugging her wrist free, the outline of four fingers there in angry red.

"So you had one of those new-age Dominants, I'm guessing?"

Parker was already putting on her dress.

"Don't go, Parker, please... I can take you to new heights. Show you how the real community works."

She yanked the fabric over her head and struggled it down over her torso.

"Thank you, but I really don't think—"

Brenna cut her off. "You were right, trust is important, but what you need to learn is to trust me to make the right calls for you... To know when to push you."

It was all wrong.

"Sit down and we'll have another drink and we can talk more. I can help you really understand, Parker."

Alarm bells were blaring in her head, and she snatched her purse from the table. She left the room and headed back down the hall she had entered by, praying the front door was unlocked. Mercifully it was, and with it flung open, one foot on the stoop, the fear subsided enough for her to turn and face the woman who had followed her out.

"This isn't going to work for me. Thank you for your time."

She left with her head held high, ignoring the protests and pleas that continued from the front door, as she slid down into her car and drove away.

Only after she had made it a street away, a block away, a town away did she pull to the curb and cry.

Chapter Eighteen

HER PHONE VIBRATED against her nightstand again, and she let it ring. Marion had called on and off all day. Parker had sent her a quick text last night to let her know she was home and it didn't work out, but she hadn't wanted to go into it any further, to dissect all the ways Brenna was completely wrong for her, how she wasn't Kristina.

Reading a sentence for the third time, she blew out a breath as finally the vibrating stopped, and forced herself to focus. This was nice, relaxing. She was in bed by eight with a glass of wine and a book she'd been meaning to read for years. It was quiet and simple, and exactly what she needed to recharge. She'd barely made it two lines down before the phone rang again.

She slammed the book facedown to keep her place, yanked it from the nightstand, and accepted the call.

"I told you I would call you tomorrow, Marion!"

She tried to keep the worst of the venom out of her voice, but really, she was a grown woman, and it was well within her rights to want to just...keep things private for once. Marion sucked in a breath down the line, and Parker knew she was going to let her have it.

"Not Marion."

Kristina.

Her stomach flopped, and everything in her chest contracted, a hot pang of adrenaline shooting through her, leaving her bolt upright in bed.

"What the fuck were you doing with Brenna Carl?" The question was a hiss, and the hope that had sprung into her chest, hot and traitorous, twisted.

"I'm sorry, but how is that your business?"

There was a terse silence down the line, and then a soft rhythmic click that sounded like...

"Are you driving?"

She shouldn't care. Kristina huffed out a breath, and Parker heard the roar of the engine as she gunned it harder. Parker sprung out of bed without thinking and studied herself in the bathroom mirror, only static and the sound of the car over the line. Surely Kristina wasn't coming here... Even as she fixed her hair, she told herself it was stupid to expect it.

"You're always my business, Parker."

The words were soft and lightly slurred, and any thoughts of how she looked were forgotten.

"Krissie, have you been drinking?"

"Are you still seeing Brenna?"

Sitting on the edge of the tub, her feet cold against the tile in her bathroom, Parker tried to calm the worry gripping her. Kristina had no right to ask her anything, but the thought of her drinking and driving...

"No, it was a one-time thing. It didn't work out."

A stream of curses, half-recognizable, the rest she assumed were Spanish, spilled down the phone.

"Did she...respect your limits?"

She was speaking just a fraction too slow, her voice too rough, the words not quite cadenced right.

"Kristina, nothing happened between us. Have you been drinking? Are you driving? Answer me, please."

"Nothing happened." She laughed, and it was cold, bitter. "If nothing happened, then tell me why the fuck you were in your underwear in her living room yesterday?"

The words were punctuated with the slam of a car door, and despite herself Parker rushed from the bathroom to her bedroom window, breathless with hope and relief that turned to dust when the street outside was dark, her driveway was still empty.

"How do you know what I was doing yesterday?" She trusted Kristina, still, implicitly, always, but the skin on the back of her neck prickled with discomfort.

"Because that cunt is posting all over Facebook about her new submissive and she has cameras in her fucking house, Parker."

Her chest constricted.

"My job..."

She choked the words out, already imagining the dean, her students, her brother seeing those images... She was shaking as she sunk down to the carpet.

A crash came down the line followed by another stream of expletives.

"Relax, I took...fuck...I took care of it. She only posted in the Pandora Doms Facebook group, and it's already been removed. She'll be blacklisted by the agency by morning, and it won't go any further."

How had she been so stupid, so reckless? She had waltzed into that situation so carelessly, so easily, expecting it all to be just like Kristina, or hoping for it. She could have lost her career, her dignity...

"Parker..." Kristina's voice was soft, and Parker swiped roughly at the tears spilling down her cheeks. Nothing was like Kristina, and sitting on the floor with fear and relief and a million emotions pouring through her chest, she let herself close her eyes and listen to the soft sound of her breath, let herself enjoy this, before morning came and again, Kristina would be gone.

"Sweetheart, it's taken care of. You're going to be fine, I fixed it, you're fine..."

She was half talking to her, and half to herself. Kristina was drunk, there was no denying it, and Parker was torn between anger that she had driven and resentment and aching, burning, maddening longing for her.

"Why would you do that? What do you care?" Her voice was as wet as her cheeks. She told herself it didn't matter. Kristina wouldn't remember any of this in the morning anyway.

"You know why." The answer was dark, and it was all she offered before she fired back a question of her own. "Are you looking for a new Domme?"

Parker sucked in a breath, pressing her fingers to her eyes.

"I don't know, Krissie."

She was tired, and the pieces of her that had been so tangled up with Kristina, the ones she had scrubbed raw over the past six weeks trying to remove her, ached and burned and bled anew.

"Sweetheart..." It was soft and sad, an endearment and a plea, and finally, it broke her.

"Don't. Just don't, Kristina. You either want me or you don't." She swallowed hard. "I appreciate you getting the picture taken down, but you... You didn't want me." She choked down a sob, feeling pathetic.

"I always wanted you." The reply was fierce, and Parker's own anger, her hackles, rose in response. Her chest expanded and her wings opened, and she dared to demand it, to ask for it, to lay it out even in the face of the rejection she knew would come.

"Then come and fucking get me."

Silence hung down the line.

"Exactly." Exactly. Nothing had changed. Kristina was still the same complicated, enigmatic treasure she had fallen in love with, and she was still too scared to acknowledge her feelings.

Parker almost hung up the phone, but something stopped her.

"Were you drinking and driving?"

"What do you care?" She grit her teeth as her own words were parroted back to her, sullen.

Parker heard the pop of a cork, and the trill of liquid against glass.

"Kristina, are you still drinking? You're wasted!" She hadn't meant to sound so incredulous.

"Yes, Mistress, I am. Are you going to come over here and spank me for it?" The words were all sarcasm and disdain, childish in a way Parker had never heard her. This was descending, spilling into something she refused to let be her last memory of her.

"Please take care of yourself, honey." She hadn't meant to let the endearment slip out, but it was too late, and panicking, she rushed on. "Good night, Krissie."

She ended the call before she could be convinced otherwise.

A TEXT MESSAGE from Marion flashed across her screen, and pausing packing up her desk, Parker picked it up. A picture of the nursery greeted her, painted a pastel purple and sea-foamy green, all the furniture in place. A week had passed since the phone call, and Marion had been her lifeline, listening to her cry the next morning about Brenna, the photo, Kristina, all of it. LiLing was a saint. Parker had painted those walls along with them, wedged between them, torn between feeling grateful and guilty. She was never an intruder, not with them, but part of her knew she didn't belong there either. It was their moment, and she was just an eternal added extra.

She typed back a quick message about how amazing it looked and turned down the invitation for dinner that had followed. Marion was seven months pregnant and glowing, if grumbling some too. This time was theirs, and she had to start standing on her own feet again.

She shoved her phone into her jacket pocket and packed the last of her papers into her briefcase, trying hard not to think about Kristina—what she was doing, who she was with, if the drinking was a one-time thing.

A foot scuffed in the doorway to her office, and that same stupid, hapless hope shot her in the gut, and when she looked up to greet the dean's eyes, it died a death just as painful as it always was.

"Professor Freeman."

She smiled, shouldering her bag and meeting him halfway into the room.

"What can I help you with?"

He adjusted the stack of books under his arm and motioned out to the corridor. She walked with him, heading back toward the entrance of the building.

"I just wanted to let you know the new library wing looks to be ready to open within a month."

Her reply came a second too late. It took her just a little too long to wade past the thoughts, the memories of the benefit, of her.

"That's... That was certainly fast. I can't wait to see it."

She offered him a beaming smile, forcing herself to live in the present.

"Yes. How is your partner doing?"

Her blood turned to ice, her words frozen in her throat, choking her. He didn't seem to notice that she'd fallen out of step with him for just a moment, too caught up in the excitement of the development.

"I'd really come to ask if you'd consider cutting the ribbon on the new wing?"

It was too much too fast, and she managed to squeeze out a little laugh she hoped sounded surprised and flattered.

"Miss Diaz made a very large donation, and you've made a wonderful contribution to the English faculty over the years. I think it would be very fitting to have you as a part of the ceremony." He finally looked at her, and her eyes must have bugged wide, as immediately his free hand was on her arm, reassuring.

"It will be small, just a few of the board, maybe some pictures for the school publication and website, very informal."

She swallowed and nodded, smiling woodenly as her heart sank. He must have sensed her hesitance.

"Think about it and let me know?"

She agreed she would, stumbling through the politest goodbye she could manage before she rushed for her car.

Finally alone, she let her head rest against the wheel, spinning.

I always wanted you.

She sat back and yanked out her phone. Her finger hovered over Kristina's contact.

I could call her. Somehow she knew Kristina wouldn't deny her. If she asked to start over, to remake their arrangement, to stop asking her for more, she'd do it. Even if it was a promise they both knew they couldn't keep. It would be that easy. She could be at her house in half an hour, her fingers tangled in Kristina's dark hair, her body pressed so impossibly close against her... And none of it would last.

Maybe she could go back, reset the cycle, but while they both wanted different things, it would be doomed to end the same way. It might prolong some of the hurt but not prevent it, and it wasn't fair to either of them.

Blowing out a breath, she locked her cell and watched the screen go dark.

It was time to move on.

Chapter Nineteen

THREE WEEKS LATER she cut the ribbon. She stood beside the dean and smiled while the cameras flashed, wearing a flattering dress, a hair shorter, the slit a little higher than the old Parker would have dared. Kristina was gone, but not forgotten. She echoed in everything, but Parker was learning to feel her presence as a gift and to stop aching over her loss. Life was good. She ran, she still loved her job, Marion's baby was due in just over a month, and she'd been on a slew of first dates that never became more, but she enjoyed them all the same.

Someone shook her hand, and the congratulations on the new library wing didn't feel bought. Kristina had written a check, and maybe that was part of the motivation for her presence at the ceremony, but more than that, she had invested her time here, her passion. She had earned this.

The dean caught her eye and waved her over, probably to meet some other important figure now the formal part of the ceremony was done. She shook hands and smiled genuinely, conscious of the way the man's eyes lingered on her appreciatively. A soft blush colored her cheeks when her phone rang, and seeing Marion's name on the screen, she excused herself.

"Is everything okay?"

Her companions must have heard the pitchy anxiety in the words, because they fell away immediately, giving her privacy.

"Yes... Well, sort of..."

Her anxiety roared.

"Are you having the *baby*?"

"What...? No, no, not that."

She had barely breathed a sigh of relief before the next fear floated forth. "Is everything okay with the baby, though, and Roland and—"

"Parker. Stop. I'm just going to say it, okay?"

Her heart plummeted, and the seconds Marion drew in a breath felt like an entire day, a whole week.

"Kristina's in the hospital."

Kristina... Marion was calling her, from pathology...

"Is she..." She stumbled to the side of the room and slipped behind one of the new stacks and out of sight. She tried again.

"Is she... Marion..." It was a whimper, tears already in her eyes.

"No! Oh God, sweetie, no, no, she's not with me. She's alive. It was Emily who came to tell me. She came through the ER. She's in neurology now. I don't know what happened or how long ago she was admitted..."

Her heart beat frenetic, her body hummed with energy, starting deep in her chest and burning its way out. It all rushed back and through her, the phone call, the drinking, a million possibilities, and the thought of Kristina, Kristina, Kristina in the emergency room.

"Parker." Marion brought her back to the present. "I just thought you'd want to know. I can try to find out—"

"No." She cut her off, certain now, already walking, rushing, running as soon as she hit the corridor. "I'm coming."

THE HOSPITAL HAD always made her feel sick, stifled. Before, it was the place where it happened, where her wife betrayed her and everyone knew. Then, it was Amanda's turf, a place where Parker was no longer welcome, a place where she didn't want to be anyway, not when she was the last to know and they all knew that. None of it mattered as she skidded through the double doors, bypassing the front desk and sliding into the elevator with a group of nurses she thankfully didn't recognize.

The floors ticked by too slowly, too many people entering and exiting, and her foot tapped, louder, louder until the woman beside her eyed it pointedly. Yet she couldn't make it still. Kristina in the emergency room, Kristina in neurology. Her brain screamed "Kristina" over and over, a million different scenarios, a constant reel of a million moments with her passed. The elevator jerked to a halt on her floor, and she was out, squeezing through the metal doors before they were fully open.

"I'm here to see Kristina Diaz."

She was breathless with the declaration as she forced herself to stop at the front desk. The woman looked up from her computer, slow, lazy in the face of what felt like her own body moving in hyperspeed.

"Miss Diaz isn't accepting visitors."

Parker grit her teeth, taking a breath and blowing it out rather than letting all her fear, her frustration, spill out on this woman who was just doing her job.

"I need to see her, please." She plastered on her best diplomatic smile. "It's important."

"I understand." It was clear from her tone that she didn't understand at all. "But Miss Diaz is not—"

"I need to speak to your department head, now." Parker let her tone cool, clipped and entitled, matching the one she had seen Amanda use so many times, the one that always got her what she wanted, because she fuck it, she didn't want to see Kristina; she needed to.

The woman sucked in a breath, nodding. "Take a seat, ma'am. I'll see if she's available." She got up and left the desk, but Parker stayed. Her skin prickled, her fingers felt numb, and Kristina was here, somewhere, in one of these side rooms, in some state of hurt… She heard talking from the door behind the nurses' station, and they were going to deny her, she knew already. Visiting was heavily restricted on a lot of the wards, save for immediate family and…

An idea sprung up and she dug through her purse. She opened her wallet and ignored the churning in her guts at the sight of her old wedding rings inside. She had planned to finally take them to be valued sometime this week, in the spirit of moving on… *Moving on.* God, that felt so long ago now, so alien when Kristina was hurt.

The cold metal of the engagement band felt foreign yet achingly familiar. Trying to ignore the weight of it, she fumbled her wallet closed, and shouldered her purse just in time to look up and greet the tired eyes of the department head.

"Ma'am, I'm sorry, but the patient you're inquiring about—"

"I need to see my fiancée, now." She spat the words, impatient. "Can someone please show me the way, or do I need to call my lawyer?"

A beat passed between the two women in front of her, and Parker saw their uncertainty in it.

"Let me go and check…" She followed the nurse's line of sight down the hall, and *of course.* She was off, moving fast, heels clicking against the smooth tile floor before they had time to go on. All the floors were more or less the same, and she remembered from the few times she'd visited with Amanda, years ago when she was still shiny enough and new enough and important enough to be included in her life here, that they all had private rooms at the very end of the corridor.

"Ma'am!"

Sneakers slapped the floor behind her and she heard them calling security, but none of it mattered. She was breathless, heart racing, frenetic energy burning through her when she threw open one of the doors at the end of the corridor.

The empty bed tore at her soul. Turning, she threw open the other door, glancing back at the ward staff who were hovering halfway down the corridor, calling back to security as they stepped off the elevator; then she stepped inside.

A hand grabbed her arm, a gun was shoved in her face, and there was a shout and a yelp, and then Kristina was in her arms, pale-faced and clinging to her, shoving the gun away from her face with one hand. Parker wrapped her arms around her and held on.

Garbled Spanish spilled back into English. "Put that away now, she's with me, she's okay..." as Parker struggled to catch up.

"Kristina..."

Kristina's eyes finally left the man with the gun, looking up at her from above shadows. Studying the split in her lip, the bruising that spilled down from under her left eye and over her cheekbone, Parker squeezed her tighter on instinct. Her hands fell away when Kristina hissed.

"Ma'am." The door burst open behind them, and two security officers stepped inside, tasers pointed at her. Looking around to the psycho who had a gun trained on her not two minutes before, Parker found no trace of the weapon.

"She's fine. She can stay."

Kristina was holding on to her, a hand possessive at her waist, though the other was across her own middle almost like she was holding herself up, together. Parker stepped up to her side, and reached out to support her gently, watching her wince as she sagged against her.

"Miss Diaz."

The nurse from the desk appeared next. "This woman..." She paused as she studied the two of them. "Your fiancée..." It wasn't quite a question, and everyone looked at everyone.

"My fiancée will be staying." Tired as she looked, humor touched Kristina's eyes at the words. Despite the bruises on her face, the blood, Parker felt some of the heaviness leave her chest.

The hospital staff filed out with an apology to Kristina, and one for another man in the corner who she hadn't noticed before. He was eyeing her shrewdly, dark eyes studying her as his face betrayed nothing. He looked a few years older than her, and Parker was just about to wonder who he was, before Kristina sucked in a breath as she moved to step back to the bed, and it all came back to her.

"What happened? Marion called me..." She followed her frantically, hovering, unsure where to touch her without hurting her, as she moved woodenly, sinking down to sit on the bed, grimacing.

"She was in a car accident," the older man supplied helpfully, the words heavily accented.

"*A car accident?*" She was shrieking, but she couldn't help it. She sat carefully on the bed beside her. "This is what happens when you drive like a...a...an idiot. You could have been killed, look at you..."

Kristina had been trying to interrupt her, saying her name over and over, but panic was bubbling up in her chest and this had all happened so fast and...

"Parker."

A cool hand was on her arm and dark eyes were on hers, and she saw the pain the movement had caused.

"I'm fine... I'm fine, really."

She was finally able to take a breath, to drink her in, the curve of her lip and the shape of her chin, the black of her lashes against the bloody purple of the bruises on her face.

She could have lost her. The thought roared in her head. She loved her, then, now, always. The words rang in her ears, and the moment was swelling, heavy, spilling, everything raw and open and pulled to the surface. Kristina's tongue moved across her bottom lip, and Parker drew in a breath, rough with nerves and sweet with anticipation, because she couldn't live in a world where Kristina didn't exist.

"Shall we talk about the engagement now?"

They sprang apart guiltily at the interruption. Parker's cheeks flamed as she remembered they weren't alone in the room. Kristina recovered first.

"Caesar, wait outside."

The guy with the gun disappeared on command, and Parker eyed him as he left them alone with the older man.

"Papa, she was just—"

"Is this what all this has been about? The drinking, the parties, the driving while drunk?"

Parker couldn't help herself.

"You were drinking and driving again? Krissie, you could have been killed... You could... Do you have any idea how irresponsible... What were you thinking?"

Thoughts slipped into and over each other, and Kristina gawked at her, cheeks red until her eyes flitted back to the man, and Parker realized he was her father.

"I'm sorry." The apology was automatic. "I just..."

"No, please." He looked amused in the face of her discomfort. "Go on. She doesn't listen to me; perhaps she will listen to her future wife." He was toying with them both and her cheeks burned in response.

"Papa, please." Kristina was as shamefaced as Parker had ever seen her, and a part of her was gratified at the sight.

"I'm sorry." Parker cleared her throat when the words came out rough. "It was the only way they'd let me in." She yanked the ring off her finger and stuffed it in her pocket, trying to ignore the silence that had engulfed the room.

"I should go," Kristina's father said. "Caesar will stay until you're discharged. Call me from home?"

Kristina answered in soft Spanish, and Parker heard the apology in the words she couldn't translate as she studied the tiles. A large tan hand appeared and she looked up.

"Mario Diaz."

Her fingers slid into his without any real thought. "Parker Freeman. I apologize for the intrusion."

They shook hands, and then he let her go.

"No intrusion, Miss Freeman, but perhaps now you are here this...recklessness will be done, yes?"

What started as a conversation with her turned into a question for Kristina. Kristina bowed her head, sufficiently chastised, her agreement soft.

"Call me from home, Mariposa."

The door clicked closed, and then they were alone.

In the silence, Parker was catching up, wrapping her brain around all this for the first time since Marion had called her. She was here, with Kristina. Kristina had been in an accident. She turned to Kristina, whose dark eyes rose to meet her gaze. Her own fell.

"Oh my…"

She reached out, stopping herself just before the pads of her fingers made contact with the deep-purple bruise just visible over the neckline of Kristina's shirt, climbing over her collarbone and disappearing at her left shoulder.

"It's from the seat belt."

The words were quiet, guilty.

"Kristina…" She paused to wet her lips, and to try to clear the judgment from her tone. She was scared, and she wanted to lash out, but with Kristina's presence sinking into her bones, Parker let herself focus on relief instead.

"What happened?"

Kristina let out a little puff of breath that became a gasp of pain when she half shrugged.

"I wrecked my car. I called my dad before I blacked out, which is why I'm in the hospital and not in jail. I have cracked ribs and a concussion, but other than that… I'm fine."

Parker watched her breathe out the words. She didn't look fine. Before Parker could tell her as much, ask her what she had been thinking, Kristina was speaking.

"Why did you come?"

Her cheeks flamed at that, rejection burning hot in her throat, before cool fingers settled over her own, the movement making Kristina grimace, though she held her hand, tight.

"No... I didn't mean it like that. I just... Why do you care?"

The smallness in her voice when she asked the question tamped down some of the anger it incited in Parker.

"Just because it didn't work out doesn't mean my feelings changed. I still care about you. I didn't get to just click that off when you drove away that morning."

They both knew which one she was talking about, the goodbyes outside her house. Stony silence hung over them, yet Kristina didn't let go of her hand, and that spurred Parker on.

"Marion called, and all I knew was that you were in the hospital. I wasn't sure how bad it was and I...panicked and then I was driving, and I just...had to know you were okay."

She swallowed, unable to meet Kristina's eyes.

"Why did you meet with Brenna?"

"Really? Of all the things you could say to me right now, that's what you choose?"

Part of her felt guilty at the whispered apology she received. Kristina refused to look at her, pitiful with one arm around her middle like she was holding herself together, one hand still clinging to her own. Parker sniffed, trying to clear her head.

Silence settled over them again. She clutched Kristina's hand tight and tried to think beyond her presence, beyond those slim fingers that felt so right in her own, beyond all these things she ached for still, but could never have.

"Would you be more comfortable lying down?"

She asked the question quietly, catching Kristina's eyes shoot open, her neck straightening as she jolted awake beside her, clearing her throat.

"I don't know. It literally hurts to breathe right now. I just want to go home."

"What are you waiting for?"

Kristina unwound her arm from around herself and was halfway to reaching for a cup of water from the nightstand before Parker stopped her.

"Let me."

Untangling their fingers was almost painful, but somehow she managed it. Standing, careful not to jostle her, she retrieved the water. Kristina's eyes tracked her movement, flitting between her and the door. Parker couldn't decipher if she was hoping she'd leave, or hoping she'd stay.

"CT results, I think."

Kristina took a long swallow, and Parker had to tear her eyes away from the slim column of her throat, the bruise starting at its base and spilling bloody across her chest, violent shades of red and purple.

"Miss Diaz."

Parker's cheeks colored as the nurse from the front desk appeared in the doorway, glancing at her before her gaze fell to Kristina.

"Your results came back. Everything looks fine, but the doctor will be by in just a few minutes to speak with you and discharge you. Here's the paperwork. Could you make a start?"

Parker stood automatically to receive the clipboard and carried it back to Kristina as the nurse closed the door.

"Do you need help or...?"

Shaking her head, Kristina took the board. She balanced it with some effort across her lap and started the discharge forms.

Parker watched her write, noticing the smooth curve of her script as she wrote her name.

"Your middle name is Maria?"

When Kristina looked up at her, a light blush colored her cheeks.

"It is. Why are you looking at me...like that?"

Parker shrugged. Suddenly the right words eluded her.

"There's just...so much I don't know about you, yet I..."

She couldn't bring herself to finish.

"You know more about me than anyone in the world who isn't family." The sincerity in Kristina's voice stirred something inside her, waking it, making it dance to the siren song of hope.

"More than Mal?"

She didn't know why she asked, it wasn't important, but Kristina answered anyway.

"Yes. More than Mal. More than anyone."

The eye contact was loaded. Hurt as Kristina was, vulnerable as she looked, dark eyes suddenly warm, lips slightly parted, her beautiful face bloodied and bruised, it was so easy to want to lean in. Parker ached to kiss her, to wrap her arms around her and never let go. There was so much she didn't know about her still, and she wanted to, badly.

She wanted early morning yoga, and breakfast for dinner at IHOP. She wanted slim fingers tight on her throat and obsidian eyes on her, always.

"Parker."

It was there in her voice, just like it had always been, and she could so easily believe Kristina wanted it too. She had no idea who leaned in first, no idea when Kristina's eyes fell closed, thick lashes brushing her bruised cheek, no idea when she'd decided to wet her lips, to close the gap, to throw caution into the wind and just...

"Miss Diaz?"

They shot apart. Kristina yelped softly, the clipboard falling to the floor with a clatter.

"Ah yes, Maggie mentioned your fiancée was here. Doctor Douglas."

The woman held out her hand, and Parker rose to her feet. She grabbed the fallen paperwork first, and then straightened to shake with fervor. The blush on her cheeks felt nuclear.

"YOU DIDN'T HAVE to go to all this trouble."

Parker took her eyes from the road to look at her for just a second, before she returned them to the traffic. Broken ribs and a concussion; the last thing Kristina needed was another wreck because Parker was completely distracted by her presence.

"And who would have taken you home if I hadn't?"

Irritation simmered close to the surface as she glanced in the rearview, because she already knew the answer. Sure enough, behind them a black sedan weaved in and out of traffic, catching up until, again, its front bumper was almost pressed to her back one.

"Caesar would have—"

"Probably killed you on the drive." She cut over her, glaring again, wishing for the car behind them to disappear.

"What's the issue with Caesar? Explain it for me." There was a flash of the old Kristina in the command, and it made Parker ache down to her bones for a different time, a different them, back when she was Kristina's. She shoved the feeling away.

"Let's see. He stuck a gun in my face. How did he even get that into the hospital, by the way? Who is he, and why is he following us?"

When she risked one more glance at Kristina, she looked harrowed, hair pulled back into an unruly knot at the nape of her neck, the bruise on her cheek intensifying, dark eyes tired.

"I've said I'm sorry about the gun, sweetheart."

The words were breathed out, exhausted. Combined with the endearment, Parker instantly relented, more than a little guilty.

Streets became familiar, and by the time they were turning into Kristina's large driveway, an odd sense of nostalgia was washing over her. Caesar was already out of his car and approaching, ready to input the code into the security system. Faster, Parker stabbed the numbers, somehow gloriously justified when the gates swung open for her like they always had.

The man asked a question in quick, clipped Spanish. Kristina couldn't have answered if she'd wanted to, because they were already driving inside. Parker tried not to think about the fact she hadn't changed the code, what it meant that Kristina, who trusted so little, had trusted her like that.

When she'd rounded the car and tugged open Kristina's door, she was still sitting there, belted in and looking miserable.

"Smugness doesn't suit you."

The words came out with the ghost of a smile, a trace of humor, though she stayed frozen in the seat. Parker shrugged them off and leaned down, ready to help her unbuckle and get out, which would be an ordeal if getting her in was anything to go by.

"Miss Diaz..."

Caesar was around her in a second, already leaning over. He slid his large hand down into her car and released the seat belt before peeling it carefully away from Kristina's chest. He moved around her with so much familiarity. Parker felt her jaw working, teeth grinding, an old habit she had thought she'd quit. What was he even doing here?

Finally on her feet, a glaze of tears over her eyes from the effort, Kristina caught sight of Parker's face. Quick Spanish spilled from her lips as she stepped out of Caesar's hold, and looking chastised, he stepped back.

They started toward the door in silence. It only took two slow steps before Parker was in his place, her hands on Kristina's shoulders, holding her steady.

"Let me."

Parker reached around her, trying to ignore the achingly familiar scent of Kristina's shampoo as she took the purse from her hand. Parker found her familiar bunch of keys and unlocked the door after Kristina pointed her to the right one. She took way more joy than she should have in slamming the door behind them in Caesar's face.

Kristina gave her a dark look, a sliver of amusement in her eyes, but didn't say anything.

Good.

Parker clicked the lock into place and followed her deeper into the house.

It was strange to be back there, her mind already spilling back to the first time she had walked down this hall, all the moments since. Kristina pinning her against the front door, her first tentative steps into the living room, the way those dark eyes had watched her, burning with amusement as she'd realized Kristina was going to be her Domme, the hot breath on the back of her neck the very first time she'd made her come.

"What are you thinking about?"

She was looking up at her now, pale and tired as she struggled to find a comfortable position on the sofa where they'd made love, before it all went horribly wrong.

"Nothing." It hurt to deny it all, to turn it all to dust, but what's past was gone.

Kristina watched her with guarded eyes as she hovered, and Parker knew she didn't buy it.

"Do you need a drink or anything?"

Kristina's eyebrows shot up, interested.

"Water, Krissie, Jesus... After all this."

"Enough." The snap surprised Parker, and her lips clicked closed automatically. "Come and sit down, please." It wasn't quite a request, but it was gentler, and it was still enough to make her spine tingle all the way down to her toes as she did.

Kristina studied her for a long moment, and Parker studied her in return. Quiet, still, the same pull, the longing that had found her in the hospital returned, and here, in the house that had just been beginning to feel like home when she'd lost it all, it was worse than ever.

"You look beautiful. Did I tell you that yet?"

The words were careful. Delivered as confidently as always, but there was a sliver of restraint in them, and Parker sensed it easily. She thanked her, smoothing her hands over the modest dress she'd picked out this morning for the library opening. It felt like forever ago now.

"Where were you when Marion called?"

She shot her an accusing glance, and Kristina held her gaze, defiant.

"I was busy." It was childish and she knew it, but a little part of her wanted to let Kristina believe there was someone else, another Brenna, another her. That life had gone on after her. If the thought of her with someone else still made her jealous, then good. It was clear from her stormy expression it did.

"I have to shower." She was as cool, as detached as Parker had ever heard her, and she knew she'd struck a nerve.

"Let Caesar in on your way out."

Parker's hackles rose at that.

"What, you like guys now? Is that why you didn't want to be with me?"

Kristina's face cracked, going from stormy to thunderous, as she struggled to her feet, clutching her chest, hissing.

"We've been over this. I never said I didn't want to be with you."

Parker shot up after her.

"Oh, I'm sorry, why you *couldn't*."

"You know why I couldn't." They were moving slowly back down the hall, and part of her was panicking because she wasn't ready for this to end; she wasn't ready to be on the outside again, away from her. "And Caesar has nothing to do with it. He's my driver and guard, nothing more."

Parker spluttered. "You have a bodyguard now?"

Something flashed across Kristina's face, and Parker couldn't help but think she looked caught.

"Who are you? Do I even know you at all?" Tears were spilling onto her cheeks, and she didn't know if she wanted to surge forward and kiss her or turn and run. It hurt. It still ached like it was yesterday they'd said goodbye, and now, so confusingly, maddeningly close to her, with everything so broken and twisted, she wanted to burn it all and she wanted to drown in it.

Kristina swayed on her feet, and Parker stepped up to her without thinking. She held her hips, careful not to touch her torso.

"Was any of it real?"

When Kristina's dark eyes met hers, they were wet with tears, and Parker already knew. Kristina loved her.

Her heart beat hard, and for a second, she believed Kristina was about to lean up and kiss her, and somehow they could find their way through all this together. Instead, Kristina finally stepped back, looking agonized. Parker knew she was trying to find the words to say goodbye again.

"I'm not leaving." She dropped her purse on the side table, decided, steely in her resolution as Kristina opened her mouth to protest. "The doctor said you need to be monitored for seventy-two hours, and I doubt that buffoon can even tell the time, let alone recognize the subtle causes for concern that can accompany a concussion."

Kristina wet her lips, one arm still around herself. She looked totally exhausted.

Whatever had happened between them, Parker didn't want to see her hurt, to see her suffer. Swiping her fingers across her cheeks, she promised herself she would stay to

make sure Kristina was all right, nothing more, and then...
She didn't let herself think it, not yet.

"I'm going to run a bath for you." She strode off down the hall, leaving Kristina to trail slowly behind her.

THE HOUSE WAS quiet when Parker stepped out of the shower. She had run the bath. She'd laid out clean underwear and sweats and tried to ignore the way her heart constricted at the now-painful familiarity she had with Kristina's life. She'd turned on the coffee machine and dug around in the un-emptied dishwasher for Kristina's favorite mug, and went to the store for the low-fat creamer she insisted on when she saw she was out. Parker had also studiously avoiding running into Caesar and his stupid shiny black car that was still parked in the driveway, just barely. The sun was long down behind the horizon before she'd headed to take her own shower.

She made her way down the hall, borrowed yoga pants and a T-shirt that smelled like Kristina clinging to her still slightly damp skin, and looked for Kristina in her bedroom. Something stirred in the pit of her stomach at the sight of that wrought-iron bed frame, the familiar gray sheets. Memories assaulted her like physical touches, crawling over her toes and winding around her ankles as if they'd twisted in the sheets, up and up her calves like the drag of smooth fingertips, cold over her fingers like the iron in her hands, all swirling and settling in the pit of her stomach, the ghost of so many nights spent here, some of her happiest, freest, wildest ever. She turned and rushed back down the hall.

Parker was breathless when she found her. Whether it was from the memories or the sight of her she didn't know. Dark hair fell across her face, her body propped up at an odd angle against the arm of the sofa, the dim light of the lamp illuminating her sleeping form.

Finally, Parker felt like she had a moment, time just to breathe Kristina in, to appreciate being back in her orbit, from the dark place so far from the sun that had become her life without her. She crept forward and sat beside her, taking the throw from the back of the oversized sofa and tucking it around them both. Kristina was small like this, still, as beautiful as she had been in any of their moments. Parker had fallen in love with her for all her brazen confidence, for all her cool commands and sexual prowess, and the new outlook on life she had shared with her. Yet studying her now, she knew she had fallen in love with this side of her too, the side of her she could never quite touch. Something smaller and less sure lived underneath Kristina's dominant persona, and all the moments, the soft kisses and the teary confessions, where it had reared its head, Parker had loved it just as much.

Amanda had been the known, the planned, the expected. Kristina was everything beyond, yet somehow, Parker felt she belonged with her more than she ever had with Amanda.

Kristina's hair was silky between Parker's fingers as she brushed it back from her face. Her thick lashes brushed her blanched cheeks before Kristina opened her eyes to catch her.

"Parker?"

She nodded, swallowing the lump in her throat.

"Think you can make it to bed?"

Kristina groaned.

"At least scoot down a little bit so your neck isn't sore in the morning too then?"

Complying, together, they worked Kristina's battered body down and sideways until she lay on the sofa, her breaths shallow from the pain. Parker made a mental note to do some research on broken ribs. She had no idea if this level of pain was normal. By the time she spread the throw carefully over her, Kristina's eyes were already closed.

Forcing herself to stop hovering, Parker turned, not ready to spend her first night in the house in the guest room.

"Parker."

It was barely a whisper, but when she looked back, Kristina's eyes were on her. If Kristina had known what she wanted to say, it must have died on her lips. Silence stretched out, but somehow, Parker understood. Sitting herself down on the carpet by the sofa, she reached up slowly and carded her fingers through Kristina's thick hair.

"Go to sleep, honey. I'll be here."

Kristina closed her eyes, a long sigh leaving her lips. Parker's already-broken heart shattered.

Chapter Twenty

SHE WOKE COVERED in the same throw she had tucked around Kristina the night before. When Parker opened her eyes, blinking in the bright light from the long window, Kristina was staring down at her, her expression unreadable. A joke about IHOP for breakfast was on the tip of Parker's tongue, yet she couldn't quite bring herself to make it, excusing herself to the restroom instead.

When she returned, two steaming mugs of coffee and a bottle of pain pills in her hands, Kristina was still sitting there, and she looked haunted.

"Hey."

She set Kristina's mug, fancy creamer and all, down on the coffee table beside her and sat at the opposite end of the sofa. The strangeness of it all swallowed her—being back in the house, the familiarity of being near Kristina that hadn't managed to die, even over their time apart.

"Thank you."

Kristina's voice was scratchy, her bruises looked even worse than the night before, and Parker ached for her. Silence hung heavy, and even the warm steam from her coffee cup couldn't slice through it.

"If you want me to go—"

"That's exactly the problem. I don't." Kristina cut her off, turning to look at her, her eyes full of the intensity Parker had always known to live there. "I didn't ever want you to go."

It should be everything she wanted to hear, but it was just exhausting because she knew this road, knew where it would ultimately end.

"What do you want from me, Kristina?"

She hadn't meant to sound so tired, and as the impact of the words landed, their emotional echo ricocheted across Kristina's face. Parker saw the shock, the rejection, the hurt, and then nothing. Her face was smooth as glass, and Parker knew that was the lockdown, because she was Kristina—Kristina who would forever be emotionally unavailable. The determination that leaked into her fine features next surprised her.

"I moved to America when I was four." Kristina's voice wavered though it was toneless, matter of fact. "Before that I lived in Guaymas, in Northwestern Mexico, in an orphanage."

Her hands shook and Parker wanted to stop her, but the profoundness of the moment stole her breath to say the words.

"My parents adopted me and Luis, my brother. I was nine when my mom died, and Luis moved back to Mexico when he turned eighteen. I was thirteen then. I already told you I knew I would inherit the family business from the time I was fifteen, and I met Calvin when I was seventeen."

"Kristina..." Parker reached across the sofa, ready to stop her, because all of it felt like a confession made under duress.

"Let me finish." The Kristina she knew rang in the command. "Please, Parker, let me finish because I don't know if I'll ever be able to make myself do this again."

Heart squeezing painfully, Parker sat back in her seat, holding Kristina's eyes until they looked away.

"I was always different." The words were still toneless, as if she read them from a script. "It was hard for me at school, trying to learn English as well as everything else; then Mom died and Luis left. All I had was Logistica, and my dad, he believed in me so much, even then. But somehow, this validation from someone else, the attention from Calvin...it got to me; he got to me. He made himself so important in my life, and then used that importance to slowly and categorically dismantle me."

She sucked in a big breath.

"I didn't know liking girls was an option. I didn't know there was anything other than him, because by the time he was done twisting me..."

Parker's heart broke when Kristina blinked back tears.

"After a particularly bad hospital visit when I was nineteen, my dad found out what was happening and put an end to it. And I just...drifted."

Kristina swallowed hard.

"Like my life was this knitted blanket, and it was blue, then one day someone came along with this thick needle and stitched red all through it, in and out and everywhere until there was almost no blue yarn left that you could see." She licked her lips, clearly uncomfortable.

"One day out of nowhere, all the red just disappeared, in a split second." She kept her eyes on her lap, tracing a pattern on the side of her now cold coffee mug, over and over.

"Even though the red was gone, the blue blanket wasn't the same. There were all these...holes where the needle went through, where the red used to be, and there was nothing left to fill them. He made all these holes in me and they just...stayed."

A tear finally spilled over, rolling down her cheek. She let it fall, and Parker ached.

"So when I was twenty I found the agency, and Mal, and I learned how to start to fill the holes, on my terms, in a way I found acceptable—a way *I* could control. And it really worked."

A sob cracked the words, and Parker scooted across the space between them.

"It worked until you."

"Kristina..." An apology hung on her lips, for everything she had just learned, and for the damage she had done to Kristina's delicate, if dysfunctional, lifestyle before her. "I never meant to hurt you. I was never supposed to fall in love with you either. I could tell you every single reason it was not what I planned or expected."

Her voice was thick with tears, and she was grateful when Kristina spoke.

"I don't think anything about me was what you had planned or expected. I remember how you tried to run from me that first day."

They shared a laugh. It was teary and tentative, but hope exploded somewhere deep in Parker's chest anyway.

"And I remember how you made me stay." She blushed as she spoke, feeling like they'd somehow come full circle, back now in the room where it had all begun.

"So if I wanted you to stay again, all I would have to do is..."

She wiggled her fingers, and the embers of playfulness in Kristina's tired eyes still made Parker burn. She laughed, soft but sad.

"I think it would take a little more than that this time, Krissie."

The admission hung between them, and Parker knew they stood on a precipice, the edge shimmering dangerously close. Her heart beat hard because she didn't know if Kristina would turn and run again, or take her hand and jump.

When Kristina reached for her hand, her slim fingers shook.

"I don't want to be scared anymore, and I don't want to watch you walk out of my life again."

Everything in Parker's chest was crushingly happy and sad and torn.

"You can't say that just to keep me if you still don't want—"

"I'm saying it because I want to move on, because I'm tired of being controlled by the fear that the minute I let someone in beyond this criteria of what I find acceptable they're going to use the way I feel about them to hurt me."

The hand in hers shook still.

"I'm in love with you, Parker. I've been in love with you since... I don't even know when. I'm sorry—"

Parker cut her off. "Do you trust me?"

The answer came quick and quiet, and enough. "Yes."

Parker leaned forward and kissed her.

SOME THINGS CHANGED, others didn't. Parker was breathless by the time they pulled up to the big house; the gates cracked open for them, the driveway lit against the backdrop of night. Kristina still drove like an idiot.

She drummed the wheel with slim fingers, impatient, her eyes fixed on the wrought iron as it parted. Parker's gaze drifted down to a pale stain on the arm of her girlfriend's black shirt.

"Looks like you have a little something there, Auntie Krissie."

Kristina smiled.

They'd all been equally surprised by how well she'd taken to the title Roland had bestowed upon her at their second meeting with barely more than a glance and his sticky little hand on her expensive suit jacket.

Realizing she was being watched, Kristina's expression broke.

"What?"

"Nothing."

Parker loved her like this, light, playful, content, even as the car lurched forward entirely too fast, the garage door barely up before they were screeching to a stop inside.

Kristina turned to her, her eyes questioning again.

"I just never foresaw this. You helping me babysit, covered in spit up. So domestic." The words were true but lightly teasing, and Parker watched their tone register, the interest playing across Kristina's face as she caught onto the game.

"You caught me, sweetheart. I held the baby, I played with Roland, I even went and fell in love with you. But do you know what didn't change?"

Her voice was slipping, spilling into something richer and darker, and Parker's body was already responding, excitement stirring deep in the pit of her stomach.

"No."

She left out the title she knew the situation demanded, licking her lips before she caught herself, sweet anticipation singing in her veins.

Kristina pushed a button, and the engine went silent.

"How much I absolutely love—" She turned to her, and Parker let herself burn under Kristina's gaze. "—a great glass of wine and a bubble bath on a Friday night."

The words sounded like sex, and Parker was almost ready to agree. When what she had said finally registered, Kristina was already up and out of the car, leaving Parker to rush after her, frustrated, amused, excited.

Kristina closed strong hands around her arms as she entered the house. She pushed her back against the wall, a soft breath of surprise leaving her. Kristina stepped into her space, intoxicating.

"What about your bath?"

Parker grit out the words against soft lips, her fingers already working the buttons on Kristina's stained shirt.

Kristina's lips parted as if to kiss her, and Parker's eyes fell closed in anticipation. Instead, a tongue slicked across her bottom lip before warm breath tickled her ear.

"Maybe later. I thought first you might like the opportunity to make up for teasing me?"

Head back against the wall, Kristina's body pressed against her, and her bottom lip between her teeth, heat and anticipation spilling through her, Parker couldn't help but grin.

"Yes, Mistress."

About the Author

L.E. Royal is a British born fiction writer, living in Texas. She enjoys dark but redeemable characters and twisted themes. Though she is a fan of happy endings, she would describe most of her work as fractured romance. When she is not writing, she is pursuing her dreams with her champion Arabian show horses or hanging out with her wife at their small ranch/accidental cat sanctuary.

Email: L.E.Royal@outlook.com

Facebook: www.facebook.com/le.royal.writes

Twitter: @leroyalwrites

Website: www.leroyalauthor.com/home

Other books by this author

Blood Echo

Blood Lust

Also Available from NineStar Press

Connect with NineStar Press

www.ninestarpress.com

www.facebook.com/ninestarpress

www.facebook.com/groups/NineStarNiche

www.twitter.com/ninestarpress

www.tumblr.com/blog/ninestarpress